I0718132

Wish: Aladdin Retold

DEMELZA CARLTON

A tale in the Romance a Medieval Fairy Tale series

Copyright © 2018 Demelza Carlton

Lost Plot Press

ISBN-13: 978-1-925799-12-5

ISBN-10: 1-925799-12-3

DEDICATION

This one's for Nanna, who gave me the copy of
Arabian Nights I still have, 26 years later.
Aladdin always was my favourite.

One

Maram wasn't sure she could think of any creature she disliked quite as much as a camel. They smelled like a carpet some drunkard had mistaken for a toilet, were about as comfortable to ride on as a bag of rocks, and they made noises reminiscent of a rutting man in the throes of the most violent lust imaginable. Actually, they were exactly like a lust-crazed man. The same hard muscle, the same sounds, and after a particularly energetic night, they didn't smell much better than a camel.

But the camel's look of disgust and habit of spitting in front of her made it less attractive than a well-muscled, naked man, who would give her some pleasure, while the camel only made her backside ache. And the matted carpet of fur upon its back seemed to drink the desert sands and rub it into her clothing when she wasn't watching. Thank the heavens it was a short journey from the port to the city, where her father's palace was waiting.

And a bath, an unheard-of luxury in some of the places she'd visited this trip. Oh, they'd had tubs and water and knew how to wash, but a bathhouse where a lady might immerse her whole body, or share that space with her lover? They'd looked at her like she was mad.

Perhaps she was, Maram reflected. Normal princesses stayed in their fathers' palaces until they reached an age to marry, when they meekly accepted the husband their fathers chose for them. They spent most of the rest of their lives on their backs, conceiving or giving birth to children to ensure the succession of their husband's line. A life spent in bed, their every need seen to by a host of servants. No need to travel or sit on a camel. Or even lift an eyebrow to seduce their husbands, who came to their beds every night without fail.

A small smile found its way onto Maram's face. Well, most nights they went to their wives. Some nights, they fell under the spell of a foreign princess and spent a glorious night trying to please the princess instead. Skills they could then use on their wives, or at least Maram hoped they would. Just because those married princesses lived an easy life, didn't mean they shouldn't enjoy their husbands' attentions. Childbirth wasn't an easy matter, or so she'd heard, never having experienced it for herself. So if she borrowed their husbands for a night – willingly, always willingly, for men were weak, and weaker still when subject to the strength of her seductive magic – she returned them with improvements she hoped their wives appreciated.

An enchantment of her own design, that ensured they gave pleasure to any woman they bedded. She had not yet worked out how to eliminate the faint blue glow that enveloped their man parts while the spell was active, but perhaps it did not matter, for surely their wives had seen enough of them not to need to look too closely. Maram had certainly not heard any complaints from her lovers, or their wives.

And her father reaped the benefits, in strategic trade agreements, alliances and other political favours his ambassadors asked for, but she ensured. She lifted her hood so that she could see Elcin, the ambassador she'd accompanied on this trip. He rode at the front of the camel train, of course, proud of his successful mission. Maram didn't begrudge him his pride, even if his success was mostly due to her. Other ambassadors had made her job more difficult – Hasan, the first ambassador she'd accompanied, had tried to force himself on her more than once, refusing to allow her to do what her father had sent her to do. Elcin had been a delight in comparison, and she would tell her father so.

Desert dust smudged the horizon now, and she knew she was close to home and the end of this interminable camel ride.

Sure enough, the city gates soon rose out of the golden brown sand, sentinels standing straight and tall to welcome her home.

Maram passed between them without glancing to either side, though she inclined her head to the bowing guards and peasants who lined the road to her father's palace. Even veiled and hooded as she was, covered in travel dust, her clothing marked her as the Sultan's daughter.

The Sultan who would demand her report before she could take that much-needed bath. She sighed as she glimpsed her favourite bathhouse, but she could not stop. Later, she promised herself. Along with all of Elcin's good news, she brought urgent tidings her father needed to know more than she needed to bathe. Even if she did smell of camel.

Her father was in his audience chamber, waiting for them, when they arrived. Elcin prostrated himself, but Maram merely stood back, inclining her head to the Sultan when he turned his enquiring gaze on her.

"So, tell me what new alliances you have made for me," the Sultan said to Elcin.

Not for the first time, Maram was glad for the veil that hid her face and her boredom from her father's court as Elcin recounted her political victories.

"And what of Beacon Isle?" Father asked.

Here Elcin hesitated. Not because his news was bad, but how close it had come to being so. "Beacon Isle is ruled by a woman, who calls herself a queen. Most unusual."

Elcin had not understood Queen Margareta's power until it was almost too late. Instead, he'd addressed his proposals to the queen's young grandson, Vardan, until Maram had intervened. The boy…nay, young man, for he'd proved himself more than capable in the bedchamber, had happily surrendered to her charms and left the great hall to his grandmother and Elcin.

Maram had whispered a warning to Elcin

that if he did not show the grandmother proper respect, her not-quite-of-age grandson would never be allowed to accept her father's proposals. Elcin had showed the woman more than respect, judging by his blushes the following morning. The newly widowed Queen Margareta had required Elcin to show her some favours, too, before she granted him any.

Politics was a game best played in bedchambers, Maram reflected. Or bathhouses.

"But do we have access to their harbour?" the Sultan rumbled.

Elcin bowed so low his forehead pressed against the floor. "Yes, Your Majesty. Queen Margareta was most insistent about that. She would have us forsake all other ports in the region to trade solely with Beacon Isle."

Maram's veil hid her broad smile. Margareta knew a good bargain when she saw one; she'd toyed with Elcin until she had what she wanted. Only then had she conceded to the trade agreement with the Sultan. In her place,

Maram might have done the same. Instead, she'd educated the prince who would one day make some girl a charming husband.

Something Maram herself would probably never have. Ah, but what did she need a husband for? She was a princess, and her father or his heirs would provide for her until the day she died. If she needed a man for anything, she could take a lover. Someone she chose for her own pleasure, and not just to satisfy her father's political aspirations.

"Maram?"

Maram jolted out of her reverie. "Yes, Your Majesty?" she asked.

"Do you need to rest after your journey, or will you share the evening meal with me?" Father asked.

Maram bowed. "My father does me great honour. I am quite refreshed at the thought of sharing a meal with our esteemed Sultan."

Father made a sound deep in his throat that told her he saw through her flattery, but he knew what she really meant – that she had news to share that she could not repeat in front of his court. News that would not wait, or she would not have appeared in court so travel-worn.

Her father's attendants dismissed the court, while the Sultan himself led the way to his private chambers. Chambers that overlooked the harem gardens, where his wives spent most of their lives.

As Maram herself might have, if it weren't for her mother's treason. Her mother's crime gave her a freedom she was grateful for, every day, though it had cost her mother everything.

"I keep thinking I might see your mother among them, but then I must remind myself that she is gone," Father said, settling beside a well-laid table.

"You can't blame yourself," Maram said quickly. "Yours was a political marriage. You were not to know that Mother's heart lay elsewhere. Perhaps she and her lover are now reunited in the afterlife."

Father spat out his wine. "There will be no afterlife for either of them. They are not dead, Maram, no matter what you may have been told. An enchantress or enchanter who commits treason is not put to death. They face a worse fate – a lifetime of enslavement, apart."

Maram's mouth dropped open. "You mean Mother is alive?"

Father nodded. "Alive, but enslaved to a magical object. She must do the bidding of its owner until she is freed. As long as she is enslaved, she cannot age or die."

"What of her lover?" Maram asked. She remembered Amani, a kind man who had conjured flowers and sweet treats for her. It wasn't until much later that she'd realised the man was her mother's lover.

Father shrugged. "Enslaved to an old lamp I once owned. He was supposed to do my bidding, but I grew tired of seeing his face, so I got rid of it."

Poor Amani, condemned to an eternity of slavery for the crime of falling in love with the wrong woman.

"But I do not want to think of that man, and I try not to think of your mother. Though

I believe you are more beautiful now than she ever was," Father said. "We are alone now. No need to cover your face."

Finally. She'd grown so used to baring her face while they travelled that wearing a veil once more was irritating, though it had kept the worst of the sand out while they trekked through the desert. Maram peeled off the layers of linen and dropped them in a dusty heap on the floor. She shook out her hair, and gritted her teeth as it released a small cloud of sand. "The desert will not let me rest until I have told you my news," she said. "Word in the port and at every oasis between there and the city is that Sheikh Basit wants to expand his territory. He has attacked several camps, sending slaves to market through the port. From what I can gather, the camps may have been in your territory at the time. That makes the slaves he's taken your people. If it is true, we cannot afford to ignore this."

Father pounded his fist on the table. "That grasping fool keeps sending envoys here, asking for one of my daughters to be his bride.

His ambition knows no bounds. That son of a camel herder!" He let out a stream of less polite insults that were enough to make Maram's ears burn.

"Perhaps you should send him a bride, Father," she said, selecting a slice of melon. She'd missed the fruit of home while travelling.

"Let that camel dung soil one of my daughters?" Father demanded.

Maram smiled. "I was thinking of Anahita."

Father's eyes narrowed. "Do you truly think so?"

Maram nodded. "I think it is the only way to protect your people from him." Her half-sister Anahita liked to play politics as much as Maram, though her style was more direct.

"Very well." Father bowed his head. "Was there anything else of importance that Elcin missed in his report?"

"Not really. Except that I believe he has fallen for the charms of the Mistress of Beacon Isle, Queen Margareta. Either you should send him to the isle regularly to keep the woman sweet, or you should keep him away from her altogether, and see that he finds a bride who will replace that woman in his affections."

"Should I doubt his loyalty?"

Maram thought for a moment, then said, "No, not yet. But she is a powerful enchantress, a fact she keeps hidden from many of her people, though not from me. Perhaps you should keep him away from her, after all. He is a good man. It would be a shame to lose him."

"Who do you recommend?"

"Someone sweet and shy, younger than he is. The opposite of the powerful queen. Perhaps one of my cousins. Hold a celebration feast for his return and see which of the girls cannot keep her eyes off him. A love match would suit him, I think." Maram sipped her tea, feeling the heat sink into her very bones. Oh, she had missed the tastes of home.

"It sounds like you really like this man," Father mused, not meeting her eyes. "Why not you?"

Maram laughed. "Because I am not some doe-eyed innocent who will adore him as he deserves. Besides, what would I do with a husband? I can't imagine he would allow me to travel to foreign countries, negotiating trade agreements for you. Face it, Father. I am no use to you as some man's wife. But as a jewelled courtesan, I can bring the world to your feet."

"You are still my daughter, and you deserve a reward. You have done more than my ambassador, I have no doubt, yet you ask for so little in reward. If you ever wished for a husband, Maram, I would grant your wish."

Maram moistened her lips. "You do not think I would cheat on him as my mother did to you?"

Sadness clouded Father's expression. "You are not Briska. There is too much of me in you. She pursued her passions with no care for the future, but you see as far as I do, and plan for the future you desire. Maram, I swear to you, if you wish for a husband, I will consent to any match you desire."

It was a lie, and they both knew it. Her father would only marry her off for an alliance that brought him more benefit than she did currently as his unofficial ambassador. But her life suited Maram, so she did not say so.

"Father, I promise you, the only man I want is one who will build me a palace that has its own bathhouse, an edifice to rival the grandest bathhouse in the city, but for my very own. And not even you can give me that." Maram smiled sadly. Her father's palace had been built on a plentiful water supply, but her favourite bathhouse had a spring which fed the pools inside, and no other water in the city could compare to it.

Father waved her away. "Of course, you must bathe. You are a dutiful daughter indeed to come to me before you have properly washed away the dust from your journey. I shall see to it that the Firdaus Bathhouse is closed to all but you and your attendants for as long as you like."

Maram inclined her head. "Thank you, Father. It is too late in the day now, so I shall bathe in my chambers tonight, but tomorrow…tomorrow I will accept your offer.

A bathhouse to myself for the day is reward enough, I think."

It wasn't, but for now it would do.

What man would want her for a wife, anyway? Most men wanted a virginal bride, the sort Maram wanted for Elcin. They would not want a woman who had taken dozens of lovers to her bed. Lovers who had given her pleasure but nothing else, for her healing skills were sufficient to stave off disease or pregnancy, but still. To most men, that made her unclean and not a fit bride.

Of course, if they met her and fell under her spell, no man could resist her, but she did not want a man by magical means. As a lover, maybe, but not as her life's partner.

Maram sighed. She was destined to go through life alone, taking a series of lovers, but never to truly love. At least she had the freedom to choose her lovers. Not even Anahita could claim that.

And a bath. On the morrow, she would have a bath.

Maram clapped her hands to summon a

servant to help her wash in what the palace could provide. Tomorrow she could soak, but today she could at least be clean.

$$\mathcal{T}wo$$

"I can make you rich beyond your wildest
dreams. The Sultan's daughters will mistake
you for a prince, you will be so wealthy, and
you may have your pick of them!" the well-
dressed man boasted. "I am Gwandoya, and if
you come to work for me, you will never go
hungry again!"

"That's because everyone who does, dies,"
Berk muttered.

"Really?" Aladdin asked.

Berk shrugged. "Well, whoever does believe

him enough to go work for him, never comes back."

Aladdin laughed. "Well, if I went to work for him, amassed a fortune and married some princess, I wouldn't come back, either. Who wants to sit around all day in an alley that stinks of piss?"

"That's because they stable the camels here. I worked there once. Evil things, camels. They bite and spit and stand on your feet until they break all the bones, but if you fight back, you're the one who gets thrown out," Bugra piped up. The boy was not yet a man, but Aladdin had been younger than Bugra when he started coming here looking for whatever work he could find.

"What about you, boy?" Gwandoya asked, pointing at Bugra. "What do you think of my offer?"

"What offer's that?" Bugra asked.

"Riches untold, and a princess for a bride!" Gwandoya said, his eyes lighting with unholy fire.

It was far too early in the morning for that

sort of zealotry.

"Sounds better than shovelling camel shit," Bugra said, stepping forward. "Will she be pretty?"

"Far more beauteous than any woman you have ever beheld!" Gwandoya promised.

"Hey, you don't want to do that," Aladdin said, reaching for Bugra's shoulder. "He might be taking you to sell you as a slave in the market."

Bugra shrugged off Aladdin's hand. "He promised me a princess, he did. And gold. You're just jealous you didn't accept first. When I'm a prince, I'll come back and throw you a copper coin so you can use the baths. Meanwhile, I'll have a palace of my own. You'll see." Bugra headed off with Gwandoya, leaving the other men staring in their wake.

"Think we'll ever see him again?" Aladdin asked.

"Nope," Berk drawled. Other men shook their heads.

"No one who goes with Gwandoya is ever seen again," an old man said, sadly.

"Should we tell his family where he's gone?" Aladdin ventured.

The old man shrugged. "No one to tell. His mother died last year. No one will miss him." He sighed. "Much like the rest of us. If we cannot work to keep our families fed, what use are we? We should all go with Gwandoya, for it is only a matter of time before we die unmourned by anyone who matters, for our families will starve long before us."

Some of the other men nodded in agreement, but none had the energy to argue. Perhaps none of them had anyone left to lose.

Except Aladdin, who rose from his crouch to stare down at the hopeless humanity who were the closest thing he had to friends. "Speak for yourself. My mother would mourn me. I'm not staying here, waiting to die with the rest of you. A caravan came into town last night. I heard it. I'll head down to the bazaar and see if anyone needs some extra hands to help unload the goods." Anything was better than wallowing in misery, waiting for work that would not come.

So he strode out of the alley and down the main street, toward the markets, but with no idea what to do. Such was the story of his life. His father had insisted he learn to read and write, and assess the quality of goods for when Aladdin followed in his father's footsteps as a merchant. But his father had died before Aladdin was old enough to take over the business, and his mother had sold all their goods just to survive, leaving them with nothing. Not even a trade Aladdin could follow to earn a living, for he was too old to apprentice and besides, no tradesman would take him without money to pay for his board. Money his mother no longer had.

So Aladdin walked through the market, seeing good silk and bad, brass polished to look like gold and gold so dirty it looked like cheap brass, food fit for the Sultan's table and stuff even a starving goat would turn its nose up at, but he could afford none of it. He was a merchant's son turned street rat, and his mother earned more money with her spinning than he did waiting all day to be hired for a day's labour that he was never offered.

He made it to the other end of the market without realising, only to find the street full of guards. "Make way for the princess!" one shouted, shoving a camel driver under the feet of his own lead beast.

Guards who would happily let a merchant be trampled wouldn't care if they killed some street rat, Aladdin knew, so he ducked into the nearest building – the city's oldest bathhouse. He ignored the sign that said the place was closed, and shouldered open the door. The shadows inside were cooler than the street, and he could hide here until the guards went past.

It wasn't as though a princess would enter a public bathhouse. The Sultan's precious daughters undoubtedly bathed in the confines of the harem, where no man could gaze upon their virgin beauty.

One of the guards must have seen him, though, because the door was thrown open. Aladdin hurried to find some deeper shadows to hide in. He found an alcove where the staff kept the towels, and ducked behind a towering pile of cloth. Surely no one would look for him there.

"You may go," a deep feminine voice said grandly. A voice Aladdin heard in his very soul.

Booted footsteps trooped outside at her command.

A princess who used a public bathhouse? This he had to see. Unable to resist, Aladdin peeped around the towels.

A veiled woman stood beside the pool while her female servants busied themselves fetching cloths and bowls of water to bathe their mistress before she immersed herself in the mineral bath.

One came into his alcove, and Aladdin had to dive behind the towels again, though he doubted the serving girl saw him in the dark. But if the princess was going to bathe, he'd best get out before someone saw him. He couldn't have picked a worse hiding place if he'd tried. Aladdin pressed his eye to a crack in the shutters, hoping the streets would be clear enough to allow him to escape.

No such luck. The street was filled with the

princess's guards, who would capture him the moment they saw him. Peeping at the princess, however unintentionally, carried a death penalty they wouldn't hesitate to carry out.

So he had to stay put, and wait the woman out. Once everyone left, then he could leave.

He settled on the tile floor. It was more comfortable than the alley where he'd spent more days than he could count.

"There. Leave me. I will summon you when I have need of you." The princess's voice echoed through the bathhouse, amplified by some sort of magic so that it seemed she spoke beside him.

Aladdin crept to the entrance of his alcove again, curious.

Four veiled women bowed, then left, and Aladdin's heart stopped as he beheld the most beautiful woman he'd ever seen. The curve of her shoulders, enticing his eyes to travel down the crease of her spine to her peach-shaped bottom. His hands itched to touch her, to see if her skin was as soft as a peach. He'd eaten the fruit in his childhood, but it had been many years since he'd done more than look at them longingly in the market.

But never as longingly as he looked at this woman now. A princess he had no right to stare at, though he could not drag his eyes away as she descended the shallow steps into the pool. She ducked under the surface of the water, then came up and flipped onto her back, stealing Aladdin's breath as he caught sight of her breasts. Fruit from heaven, surely, so round and perfect. This princess's body was a priceless treasure none but the highest of men deserved to possess. Maybe not even then.

Aladdin buried his face in his hands. He deserved to die for what he'd seen. But if he did, he would die happy.

"Step out of the shadows, where I can see you," the princess commanded.

One of her attendants had stayed, Aladdin guessed. He ducked back behind his towels, where the woman would not see him.

"Do you really want me to summon my guards to drag you out? Come, now, man. You have seen your fill of me, so it is only fair that you let me at least see your face."

Aladdin risked a peek around the towels, to find the princess's dark eyes fixed on his hiding place.

She spread her arms wide. "I am unarmed, as you see. I will not harm you."

Just looking at her condemned him to death, but Aladdin knew he'd already sealed his fate. Fixing his gaze on her face, he took three tentative steps into the space before he fell to his knees, pressing his forehead to the floor. "Your Highness, my humblest apologies for my disrespect. I sought to clear the road to let your entourage pass, only to find myself trapped in here. Why does one of the Sultan's daughters do such honour to a common bathhouse?"

Her laughter was low and musical, bouncing off the walls and straight into Aladdin's heart. He never reacted this way to anyone.

"This is no common bathhouse. This is the first bathhouse built in the city by one of my ancestors. Better than anything in the palace, I assure you."

It was Aladdin's turn to laugh, and the walls boomed the sound back at him. He clapped a hand over his mouth, but it was too late. Anyone outside had surely heard him.

The princess did not sound worried. "They won't come in unless I call. They are my attendants, and they serve me."

"What kind of princess are you?" he burst out.

"The sort who entertains men alone if it pleases her, who prefers this bathhouse to the shallow pools in the harem. The Sultan has many daughters, and we have our own talents. Some of us are not destined for marriage alliances." She sounded almost bitter at this.

"Any man who saw you would be a fool not to beg for your hand," Aladdin said.

"Most men prefer other parts of my body to my hands," the princess said drily.

Aladdin lifted his startled gaze to her face. "But…I thought…"

Pain appeared in her eyes. "I am Princess Maram, a courtesan from the Sultan's court, who accompanies our ambassadors to far off countries. Sometimes I persuade the men of other royal houses to look favourably on my father's proposals. Most men find my body hard to resist, though you don't seem to struggle. Why is that? Do you prefer men?"

Aladdin's face reddened. "Your Highness, your beauty is irresistible indeed, but I am a humble spinner's son. I have grown used to not having things I desire, however ardently." As if to remind him that he had not eaten since the previous day, his stomach gave an alarming rumble.

Princess Maram's eyes narrowed. "Yasmeen, have food and refreshments brought for two," she called.

"Yes, Your Highness," came a voice from the entrance hall, but the girl did not appear.

Aladdin allowed himself to breathe again. "You are too magnanimous, Your Highness."

She smiled. "No, I'm quite selfish, actually. I am accustomed to having men stare at me hungrily because they desire me, not because they are starving, therefore your hunger must be satisfied. What is your name, spinner's son?"

"Aladdin," he choked out.

"Aladdin, which means excellence and faith. A name you share with the sultan who commanded that this bathhouse be built. I think there is more to you than being a simple spinner's son." Maram's eyes seemed to see into his very soul, and Aladdin was helpless to stop her.

For the first time, he forced himself to meet her gaze squarely. "Forgive my impertinence, Princess, but I am no more and no less than my mother's son."

She smiled. "And I am my mother's daughter, which defines me more than you know. I will forgive you, if you will forgive my poor choice of words."

Aladdin bowed his head to the floor once more. "There is nothing to forgive, Your Highness."

Three

Maram saw the boy duck into the bathhouse, and when she entered the cool space, she sent out her magic to search for him. She hid her smile when she found the boy hiding behind the towels. She would lure him out soon enough. First, she wanted her bath.

She let her attendants wash her, for the four of them made faster work of it than she could. Another time, she might have asked one to stay, to read or sing or converse with her while she soaked in the bath, but something about the boy's presence changed her mind, so she sent them away instead. Let them think she was meeting a lover. It would not be the first time.

She bit her lip, tasting blood as she cast a seduction spell on herself. The spell spread out like mist, swirling around the columns until it reached the alcove where her quarry concealed himself. She sensed his resistance, and wondered if he was younger than she'd thought. A child who did not yet know a man's urges would not respond to her spell the way a man would.

She called to him, first with her spell and then with her voice, until the combination of command and threat brought him out of hiding.

She was surprised to find not a boy at all, but a man grown, though a young one who was not much taller than her. Painfully thin, too, as though he did not eat enough. A thought that he confirmed early in their conversation, when his empty belly gave him away.

His gaze kept drifting away from her in a way she'd never seen happen before. No man could take his eyes off her when she cast a seduction spell, especially not when she stood naked before him. Yet he resisted, this Aladdin. A prophetic name for a man met in this place, built by his namesake so many centuries before.

Yasmeen brought the midday meal and Aladdin disappeared back into the alcove, not venturing out until Maram dismissed Yasmeen. In the servant's absence, Maram was forced to serve the food herself, but Aladdin thanked her so profusely for every bite that she found she did not mind.

He ate like a man who had been brought up in court, not some starving spinner's son, as he said. When he had finished, he bowed deeply before her again and said, "You have my gratitude, kind Princess. How may I repay your kindness?"

"Satisfy my curiosity," she said. "Tell me what you know of magic."

"I know nothing, except that it killed my father, and my mother sold everything we owned to prevent it from killing me, too," Aladdin said.

"How?" Maram demanded.

"She paid a witch to cast a spell on me, one that would shield me from magic." Aladdin's lip curled. "I told my mother she was wasting her money, for even if magic did exist, there was no proof that the witch could cast such a spell, or that it would work."

"How long ago was this?" Maram pressed.

"Ten years or more."

She inhaled sharply. "A powerful spell indeed, to last so long and still work."

He did not look convinced.

Maram took a deep breath, bit her lip, and cast a second seduction spell, more powerful than the first. The last time she had done such a thing, it had taken an entire troop of eunuch guardsmen to keep the three men she'd targeted from taking her by force.

Yet all Aladdin did was raise his head to look at her. No, to look at her face, an oddity in itself. "Did you cast a spell?" he asked.

"Yes. Do you feel any different?" she asked. If necessary, her guards would be here in moments, but she didn't think it would come to that.

"Your Highness has treated me with kindness, allowing me to share your meal and see beauty most men only dream about. I feel as though if I were to die today, I would die happy." He frowned. "Though my mother would not be so happy."

"Not as though you wished to…do things to me?" For the first time in years, Maram felt a blush colour her cheeks.

"Your Highness, the moment I saw you, I dreamed of more than any man deserves. What I wish is of less importance than I am, and I am nothing."

His dark eyes told her he spoke the truth as he believed it, impossible though it seemed. How could a man consider himself nothing?

She reached out. "Please, rise."

His hand enveloped hers, but he was too chivalrous to do more than grasp her hand as he rose uncertainly to his feet.

Maram moistened her lips. "Kiss me, Aladdin."

"Your Highness, I am not worthy." He stood as tall as she did, yet he bowed his head.

"What if I told you less worthy men than you have kissed me, when I did not ask them to, nor wish it?"

Now he met her gaze and anger flared in his eyes. "Then I hope your guards cut those men down, as they deserve. As they will no doubt do to me when you are done with me."

"No!" Maram burst out. "I swear they will not touch you. But…but I would like you to touch me." She shrugged out of her robe, so she stood naked before him once more.

Aladdin laughed bitterly. "Your Highness, I have done many things I am not proud of, but I have yet to sell my body, and I will not. I promised my mother when I was a boy that I would not take coin from the brothel keepers, who were very interested in me when I was younger and prettier, and I am a man of my word, even if my word is all I have left."

"Then I am not worthy of you, Aladdin, man of your word. Because I have sold my body countless times to secure concessions for the Sultan, and I have no doubt I will be called upon to do so many times more." Maram fought back tears. With his simple statement, the man had shamed her, yet he had done nothing wrong.

"Princess…"

"Kiss me. Please." Even as the words left her lips, she knew they had no power over him. He was immune to her magic, for all his pretty words.

Aladdin's hand cupped her cheek. The rough skin of a man who worked for a living touched her for the first time, but she relished it. This was real.

His face loomed close and she fought to slow her breathing as her heart fluttered like a bird within her ribcage.

His lips were gentle as they brushed hers, tentative and light like the touch of a bird's wings. His eyes were wide with something like panic, undoubtedly mirroring her own.

He'd never kissed a woman before, Maram realised.

She seized his face in both hands, and pressed her lips against his. He tasted of honey and spiced almond milk, as if the last drop from his cup still lingered on his tongue. She wanted more than a taste. Heavens help her, but kissing this man was like her need for air itself. Her head spun and her heart raced as never before. No man had ever had this effect on her.

And he was not as immune to her spell as she'd thought. His tongue rose to dance with hers, his lips moving with her like music itself. He made a sound of satisfaction, deep in his throat, as his free hand came to rest in the small of her back. Still he kissed her, stealing her breath as he breathed life into her love-starved body.

No man had ever…

"No, Princess. I gave my word." He stepped back from her, peeling her fingers gently from the hem of his tunic.

She'd almost managed to tug it up and over

his head. Who was he to resist her?

"But I want you to make love to me," Maram insisted. Making love wasn't what other men had done to her, but with Aladdin it would be different, she was certain.

"I want to free you from your slavery, selling your body for the good of our country," Aladdin replied.

Maram snorted, an unladylike sound that no other man had ever heard from her. "A princess's body is always used for the good of her country. Even the ones who form marriage alliances are brood mares for their husbands, living proof of the alliance between my father's kingdom and their husband's."

"So to free you, I would need to find you a husband who would love you, yet who has a kingdom to rival your father's, so that you could marry the man?" He raised his eyebrows.

Maram laughed. "Wealth to rival my father's, now, I think. He has all the alliances he needs, thanks to me, but he would marry me to a wealthy man if he thought the man's wealth outweighed my value to my father as an ambassador." She shook her head. No such man existed, she was certain. And if he did, he wouldn't love her. He'd want a virgin princess, not a well-used courtesan.

Yet Aladdin's eyes lit up at her words, as if they'd given him hope. "So if I were to amass a fortune, your father might be willing to bestow your hand on me? Then we could both have what we desire. You would be free, and I would be honour-bound to make love to you."

Her mouth was dry. "I wish it could be so."

Aladdin bowed low. "As do I, Princess. But you are a princess, so beautiful you put the sun and moon to shame, and I am a humble spinner's son, with not even the coin to pay you for the meal you have so kindly given me."

Maram waved away his compliments. "It is not necessary. Consider it fair payment for your refreshing conversation and company and…that kiss." She licked her lips, wanting another.

Aladdin seemed to read her thoughts and he backed away, toward the shadows from whence he had come. "My first, Princess, and I am honoured that it pleased you. I fear it will also be my last. Farewell." He disappeared into the darkness, and reluctantly she let him go.

He was just a man, and a lowborn one, at that. So why did she feel so bereft with him gone?

Maram summoned her servants to help her dress, but her thoughts were on Aladdin, the one man who could resist her spell.

Four

His thoughts filled with Princess Maram, Aladdin had to force himself to sneak out the back of the bathhouse instead of returning to her, like he wanted to.

She was a princess and he was nothing. He repeated this to himself, hoping that if he said it often enough, he would believe it. Because for that hour he'd spent in her company, he'd dreamed of more. More kisses like the one they'd shared, more such meals, maybe joining her in the bath, and…

No. She was a princess and he was nothing.

A princess who wished to be free. A beautiful caged bird who would soar, if only her father would let her.

"Did you find work today?"

Aladdin glanced up to meet his mother's enquiring gaze. He'd walked home without realising it, he'd been so deep in thought. "No, Maman. I'm sorry."

She sighed. "There must be something for you. Perhaps tomorrow you will have better luck. I have spent all day spinning, so if I take this thread to the tailor's, perhaps I will have enough coin to buy bread for your supper."

His unusually full stomach ached at the thought that he'd eaten, but he hadn't thought to bring anything home for his mother. "I'm not hungry, Maman. Save it for tomorrow, or for yourself. I will just go to bed."

But even lying on his thin straw pallet, Aladdin could not sleep. Maram and her melancholy haunted him. The perfect princess, whose kiss had awoken a longing he'd never known before.

When day dawned, Aladdin was no closer to getting the girl out of his mind. He trudged to the alley where he and the other labourers waited for work that never came. Day after day, he made the journey there, then home, in a dreamy haze that wouldn't lift. Hunger gnawed at his insides, but he ignored it.

"I can make you rich beyond your wildest dreams. The Sultan's daughters will mistake you for a prince, you will be so wealthy, and you may have your pick of them!"

Gwandoya's boasting burst through the haze in Aladdin's mind, as though he heard it for the first time.

Aladdin rose to his feet. Yes, he wanted to pick one of the Sultan's daughters. Because he dreamed of nothing else but Princess Maram.

"What about Bugra? Did you make him rich, so he married some princess?" Berk asked. "Is that why you need someone new?"

Gwandoya shrugged. "The boy made his fortune so quickly, he now has more gold than he can carry. He has no desire to work for me any more. Will you be next?"

Berk spat on the ground at Gwandoya's feet. "Not me. I'm not crazy."

"What about you?" Gwandoya looked Aladdin up and down, no doubt seeing what the other men did — that Aladdin was not strong enough for hard labour. Too many years with too little to eat had seen to that. "You will be able to eat like a king for the rest of your life if you come and work for me."

Aladdin would settle for sharing his meals with Maram. "What would you have me do?"

"Come with me and I will show you," Gwandoya said.

Berk caught Aladdin's shoulder. "Don't, man. Bugra's likely dead in the gutter somewhere, and if you go with him, you will be next."

If he didn't find work soon, Aladdin knew he'd be dead in a gutter anyway. He hadn't eaten in two days, and his mother was too tired to spin. A quick death was better than starving to death, and if there was a chance he might be able to free Maram…

"So be it. I shall take my chances," Aladdin

said. He dropped his voice to a whisper that he hoped only Berk would hear. "If I survive, I swear I will return here, if only to tell you the truth of what happened to Bugra and the others. If I do not…please tell my mother that I love her, and my last thoughts were of her." Whatever happened, he would no longer be a burden on his mother, for her spinning was enough to support her alone without him.

Berk looked like he wanted to say more, but he pressed his lips together and nodded. "May you have better fortune than the rest of us."

Gwandoya clapped Aladdin on the shoulder. "Good boy! You will be rich, you shall see!"

Aladdin wanted to believe him, so he hoped, but in his heart, he dreaded what would come next. Anything that made a starving boy rich had to be unpleasant. Otherwise, why would Gwandoya share such riches with anyone?

Maram trudged back to her apartment, vowing not to return to the bathhouse unless he was there. Somehow that one encounter with Aladdin had left the place empty of all joy for her. She had returned every day, yet he had not. She wanted, no she needed to see him again. She'd been touched by so many men, but that one kiss from him had burned through her memories of all of them so that only he remained.

Who was Aladdin? More than some simple

spinner's son. More than any man she'd ever known...they'd shared one moment, but that moment was everything.

"Did you put him up to it?"

Maram blinked. Two hulking shadows bracketed her favourite couch and the dark-clad figure who reclined upon the cushions.

"I'm still in mourning, you know," Anahita said, throwing herself down in a picture of despair.

Maram smothered a laugh. "In mourning for which husband? Do you even remember his name?"

Anahita sat up indignantly. "Of course I do. It was...um, Abd-something-or-other. I think. Oh, what does it matter? He never wanted me to address him by his name. I was supposed to call him Master, like I was a slave. Me! It is not fitting to speak ill of the dead, but that man..."

"Is not mourned by anyone, least of all you," Maram finished for her. "Father has a problem with Sheikh Basit. He is attacking the outlying towns and camps, taking our people as slaves."

Anahita frowned. "Then he is a fool, and Father does him too much honour, giving me to him as a bride. Is he at least a handsome fool?"

Maram shrugged. "I do not know. I have never seen the man. What do you care? All of your husbands meet untimely ends. One might think you drive your husbands to suicide."

"Oh, hush." Anahita flapped her hand at the nearest guard. For all that her sister never went anywhere without them, Maram had never learned their names. "Get us something to drink."

The man bowed and left without a word, while his twin folded his arms across his chest to appear even more formidable.

Anahita didn't even seem to notice. Maram would never understand why her sister favoured these two enormous men as her personal guards. They'd been a gift from her first husband, a man Maram knew deserved his untimely death ten times over.

"He cannot be handsome, or you would have kept this sheikh for yourself," Anahita said. "The gossip in the palace is that you have a new lover in the city. One you meet in the old bathhouse near the city gates." Anahita's eyes sparkled. "Who is he?"

Maram's heart ached at the mention of Aladdin. "No one." She wet her lips. "And he is not my lover. I met a man there once. I have not seen him since." But she would give everything she owned to see him again. Or for more than a kiss.

Anahita whistled. "A man who can resist you! A superior creature indeed. You must introduce me to this paragon. Perhaps he can keep me company when you go travelling again. A widow always needs so much consolation!"

"No!" Maram snapped, more sharply than she'd intended. She softened her tone as she continued, "You'll be living in marital bliss with that sheikh, I'm sure."

"Marital bliss is not for the likes of me, or you," Anahita said. "Why else would Father allow us to have apartments outside the protection of the harem?"

Maram shot a pointed glance at her sister's remaining bodyguard. Either one of them would be quite the temptation to her father's wives, some of whom had not spent a night with their husband since their wedding night. Someone who hadn't grown up in a harem might think it a place full of secrets, and it was, but secrets were the currency of the place, and they flowed as freely as coins in the marketplace. For a politician like Maram who was known to have her father's ear, nothing stayed a secret for long.

"Fate is fickle. You don't know what she might have in store for either of us. Perhaps you will find a handsome prince of a husband who will outlive you. And I..." She might meet Aladdin again, a man of vastly changed fortunes, who could marry her the way he wished to.

"You might find some prince who doesn't know the difference between a virgin and a courtesan, a man so stupid he allows you to rule in his stead," Anahita finished for her with a smile. "I know you. You would never be content to be anything less than a queen. I think you like the power you have over men when you travel to foreign lands. There are tales of queens who rule like men, I am told."

Maram thought of Queen Margareta, a world-weary widow who was lonely without her husband. "There are a few such women, and their lives are not easy. I would not aim so high. But sometimes it would be pleasant to be loved."

Anahita laughed. "As opposed to just being desired? You speak of that thing all the crusader knights long for. What do they call it? Some sort of divine cup? Or is it a bowl?"

"The holy grail," Maram said. "And no one knows what it truly is. They speak of a story about a knight named Perceval, or Gawain…ah, I forget. It is a favourite among foreign courts. The object is a myth, no more."

"Ah, there is always some truth in old tales, even if it is hidden deep. There are men who love their wives above all else." Now Anahita looked wistful.

"Those men are not princes, or men with

power of any kind, then," Maram said gently.

Anahita grinned. "Not powerless at all. He must have the power to please you, surely?" She pumped her hips like a rutting man might, making them both blush.

"Enough about men. They are poor gamblers, for they never bet anything of value. I have new jewels and trinkets from my travels and I'm sure you have gifts from your latest husband that you haven't yet lost in a game of chance. What say you to dice, or a round of chess?"

"It has been a long time since I have played chess. I suspect you are after that necklace…or is it the jewelled dagger?" Anahita asked. "I must teach my men to play, so that I might stay in practice while I am with this new sheikh."

"Dice, then, for a fair match. You will like some of my new jewels, and I always did like that dagger." Maram clapped her hands, and one of her serving women fetched her dice box.

"Now you are home, we should go hunting.

I have a splendid new falcon, Merlin, who has a taste for frogs above all else." Anahita grinned as she selected a die made of green glass.

"Frogs? She sounds like a very strange bird. Has she never tasted a fat pigeon?" Maram asked, choosing a die of rose-coloured wood.

"Plenty, but if she hears a frog, she will abandon the hunt to dive for the frog. Why, I've seen her skim through the bathhouse, making all the harem girls scream." Anahita's smile turned wicked. "They screamed even louder when they saw the size of the frog Merlin had plucked from their bath."

Maram tucked her feet up under her and shivered. "I'm sure I would scream, too. I do not like frogs. Slimy creatures."

"I'm told the crusaders eat them as a delicacy at home," Anahita added. "Perhaps Merlin was a crusader's falcon."

Maram felt sick at the thought of a frog anywhere near her mouth. "Enough talk of your crazy bird. Before you cast the dice, what do you hazard?"

"What would you like best, the necklace or the dagger?"

"The dagger, for it will defend me better against frogs," Maram said.

Anahita pulled the jewelled dagger from a fold in her robes, its sheath glittering with more jewels than the blade itself. "The dagger it is, then, though I doubt you will ever use it. A blade is not your style, sister. You are far more subtle than that."

"When men have had too much to drink, subtlety is lost on them, and a woman has need of a dagger," Maram said.

Anahita nodded. "You should train with me and my men one day, so that you might better defend yourself, dagger or no. For the times when a guard is not close enough to call."

Anahita's eyes met Maram's in shared pain. Both had known the violence of men, and neither wished to be a victim again.

Maram broke the silence. "So you bet the dagger, sheath and fighting lessons with your men. I will counter with an amber comb, gifted to me by the king of Kasmirus."

"Just a comb? My dagger is worth more than that," Anahita scoffed.

Maram pulled the comb from her hair and laid it on the table. "Ah, but this comb is immune to dragonfire. A dragon roasted the princess wearing it, crisping her hair to ash before it ate her, but the comb is untouched."

Anahita's eyes widened. "Did you see the dragon?"

Maram flashed an enigmatic smile. "If you want to trade for tales of foreign lands, you must increase your bet."

And so the game began.

Six

Gwandoya led Aladdin out of the city, to where he had tethered a couple of camels. Aladdin glanced apprehensively at the large beasts with hooves as big as his head.

"Have you ever ridden a camel before, boy?" Gwandoya asked.

Aladdin shook his head, not trusting his voice. He might emit an unmanly squeak.

Gwandoya barked a command at the beasts, and they both knelt down on the sand. "Climb on here, and hang on here," Gwandoya said, pointing. He waited for Aladdin to obey before he nodded slowly. "Good." He climbed aboard his own animal, then barked another order that made the animals rise to their full height once more.

Aladdin grabbed for the hairy hump in front of him to stay on the beast. "Maybe we could walk instead?" he asked weakly.

Gwandoya laughed. "And how will we carry anything back, hmm? These camels can carry very heavy loads – more than you, I think, boy. And we will reach our destination faster with them, oh yes."

"Where is our destination?" Aladdin asked, but Gwandoya didn't seem to hear him. Instead he urged his camel into motion and Aladdin had to hang on for dear life. How could something so huge move so fast? Surely its teeth were rattling in its head, like Aladdin's own.

An eternity later, when Gwandoya slowed to a halt beside an oasis, Aladdin pried his cramped arms off the camel's hump. When the animal lowered itself to the ground, Aladdin slid off into the sand. He staggered toward the water. "Is this our destination?" he croaked.

"Of course not, silly boy. This is where we stop to drink," Gwandoya snapped, before hitching his smile back up. "Drink your fill, for we have far to go until nightfall."

Aladdin's heart sank. "On the camels?" He swallowed and nodded. "Of course, on the camels. As you said, we will get there faster."

Gwandoya eyed him. "You learn fast. Maybe you will do better than the others."

The others who had died, Aladdin thought before he could stop himself. He forced a smile. "So I will get so much gold the Sultan will give me two of his daughters as wives?"

Gwandoya seized Aladdin by the shoulders and shook him. "Not the gold. Don't touch the gold." He released Aladdin. "There are other kind of wealth, things far more valuable than gold."

Aladdin opened his mouth to ask what, but then he closed it again. Gwandoya had talked about Bugra having more gold than he could carry…and now Aladdin couldn't touch it? Did that mean gold had killed Bugra, or something else? Something that owned the gold, perhaps? Aladdin had heard tales of dragons, but he'd never seen one. He wasn't sure he wanted to, either. Not if it would be the last thing he saw.

Gwandoya took out a parcel of food and proceeded to eat his fill. Aladdin watched him with his belly growling, wishing he had the courage to ask for some from his new employer, but he didn't dare. What the man had unwrapped didn't look edible at all. If Aladdin wasn't mistaken, Gwandoya was happily crunching through a handful of large bugs. Aladdin might be hungry, but he wasn't that hungry.

"Didn't you bring food, boy? Here, have one," Gwandoya held out his hand.

A closer look only confirmed that they were indeed beetles and what looked like the most enormous crickets Aladdin had ever seen, mixed with salt and spices.

"I'm not hungry," Aladdin lied, waving the creatures away. "I am eager to start work." And finish riding this benighted camel, he thought but didn't say.

Gwandoya brightened. "Good. Then we shall go, arrive by sundown, yes?"

Aladdin swallowed. "Yes."

Seven

By the time Gwandoya called a halt again, Aladdin was ready to leap off the camel with the sincere wish never to ride one again. Whatever flesh he'd had on his backside had been bounced off by the crazy animal's gait between the oasis and what looked like a pile of boulders.

Aladdin would have no trouble when he tried to obey Gwandoya's order not to touch the gold, because who would leave anything of value in such a desolate place? There wasn't even any water here to justify stopping.

Gwandoya grinned, his teeth surprisingly white in the afternoon light. "We are here, yes?"

Aladdin wasn't sure how to answer, so he didn't bother.

Gwandoya led Aladdin to a rock that didn't appear any different to the others, then knelt beside an old fire pit. He took a leather flask from his belt and poured the contents over the half-charred timbers. Then Gwandoya pulled out a tinderbox and set about rekindling the fire.

Aladdin considered telling the man it was pointless to attempt such a thing with damp wood, but nothing this man did would surprise him any more, so Aladdin sat down on a nearby stone instead.

The fire flared to life faster than any Aladdin had seen before. The liquid must have been lamp oil, Aladdin realised. Gwandoya spread his arms wide and began to chant in a language Aladdin didn't recognise as he danced about the fire.

For a moment, Aladdin thought he saw wisps of smoke rising from the man's hands, but he shook his head. He must be imagining it. Except the smoke was thickening until he couldn't deny it was real. Sparks jumped between the smoke clouds, like nothing he'd ever seen before. And still Gwandoya chanted.

The man was a magician, Aladdin realised, dread clenching at his stomach. Aladdin had heard stories about dark magicians who used blood to cast spells. Was that why he needed Aladdin – to provide the blood in this unholy ritual? Is this how the other men had died?

The smoke cloud surrounding Gwandoya streamed toward the stone, taking the vague shape of a man, though a giant man. The smoky figure grabbed the stone and pushed it to the side, revealing the dark entrance to…what? The underworld?

Gwandoya didn't look surprised. He had done this many times, Aladdin guessed. But not enough to succeed in his dark purpose, which was why he needed Aladdin.

"We're going in there?" Aladdin asked.

"No, we are not."

Aladdin breathed a sigh of relief.

Gwandoya continued, "You are entering alone. You will journey through the underground city to the treasury. Touch nothing on the way. Once you reach the treasury, and this is very important, tuck your robes up around you so that not even the hem touches the gold in there, for if you touch it, you will surely die."

Like Bugra.

"You are looking for a lamp. An old, brass lamp that will appear out of place amid such treasure."

"So why is it there, then?" Aladdin asked before he could stop himself.

Gwandoya glared at him. "It has great personal value to me."

Aladdin didn't believe a word. He might be a street rat, but he'd been raised to be a merchant, who had to know the difference between truth and lies as much as he needed to be able to sort brass from gold. "So I find this old lamp of yours, and then what? Where's the wealth you said I'd find?" Aladdin asked.

Gwandoya lifted his chin proudly. "Bring the lamp to me, and I shall richly reward you."

Another lie. But Aladdin merely lowered his eyes and nodded.

Gwandoya pulled a ring from his finger and held it out. "You will need this. This magic ring will allow you to open doors in the city."

Aladdin took the ring gingerly. It seemed real enough, the blackened silver speaking of its great age. "Do I have to do the dancing and chanting thing like you did?"

"The inner doors are not as stubborn as the city gates. You will only need to command them to open, and they will."

No chanting, then.

"Do I get a torch?" Aladdin asked hopefully. The city gates really did look like the gates to the underworld.

"There are torches inside. They will allow you to reach the treasury," Gwandoya said. "Find the lamp, and it will light your way back to me."

The lamp that wasn't his, but Gwandoya

wanted so badly he was willing to kill as many men as it took to bring the thing to him. But not enough to venture into the city himself.

"Right. Here I go, then," Aladdin said with forced cheer.

Wishing he'd stayed in his own city, where he belonged, Aladdin stepped into the dark.

Eight

"Isn't she beautiful?" Anahita marvelled as her eyes followed the falcon's flight.

"I've never seen a bird fly so fast," Maram admitted. She didn't want to watch the bird make a kill – she didn't share her half-sister's thirst for blood – but she couldn't deny she envied the bird her freedom of flight. Maram might travel the world with her father's ambassadors, but right now, she would give anything to fly, to be able to see everything in the city. Every man, too, with the sharp eyes to recognise the one she wanted. So she might ask Aladdin why he avoided her.

Maram sighed deeply. The one man she wanted, who apparently had no desire for her. Fate was laughing at her, she was certain of it.

Anahita bumped her hip against Maram's as she took a seat on Maram's stone perch. "Where does he live, your bathhouse lover?" Anahita asked, peering out over the city. "Only Merlin has a better view of the city than we do from this ridge. Why, I can see the bathhouse. Is he waiting there for you now?"

Maram shook her head. "There is no one waiting for me. Not there, not anywhere."

"Men the world over pine for you, just as you are doing now. Perhaps this lover of yours is simply fate turning the tables on you," Anahita said. She let out a piercing whistle, summoning her falcon back.

The bird circled, swooped, then circled again, not seeming to want to land yet.

Maram didn't blame her. Why would she give up the freedom of flight when she hadn't found what she sought?

But she wasn't a bird. She was a princess, a daughter of the Sultan, who did not search the alleyways of the city for a man who appeared to be a street rat, yet had higher morals than any royal prince she'd ever known. She would send a servant in search of him, Maram decided. Aladdin wasn't that common a name – she'd never known another man called that – and he lived alone with his mother, she thought he'd said. If Aladdin avoided her, his mother could not. She would send the servant with an invitation for Aladdin's mother to present herself at the palace. Maram would share a meal with the woman and ask her why Aladdin had not returned. His mother would know – mothers always did. Her own mother…Maram shut that thought down before it could fully flower in her mind. Her own mother knew nothing of her life now – such was the fate of a treasonous former Sultana.

"Oh, you stupid bird! Not another frog!" Anahita cried in dismay as the bird dived into a well.

Maram couldn't suppress a smile. Evidently she wasn't the only one who loved what she shouldn't.

Nine

For the first time, Aladdin found Gwandoya had not lied. Inside the door sat a stack of torches. He seized one and carried it back to what remained of Gwandoya's fire. It was enough to light the torch, which was all Aladdin needed. He stepped back inside the cave and set off down the tunnel into the depths.

After several turns, Aladdin found himself at a crossroads of sorts, with two paths to choose from. Gwandoya and the doorway were out of sight, so there was no one he could ask for directions. Swearing, Aladdin peered down both tunnels, but neither dusty stone passage seemed more inviting than the other.

This cave ran deeper than he'd thought. Deep enough for a man to get lost in, maybe. Was that how Bugra had died? Aladdin moistened his suddenly dry mouth. Other men might have died here, but he would not. He backtracked to where he found another unlit torch in a bracket on the wall, and lit that, too, before he headed down the right hand passage. Any torch he saw, he lit, so he'd know he'd passed this way before.

Pretty soon, the warm light of all the torches behind him made Aladdin comfortable enough to start looking around him, at what wasn't a cave at all. The tunnels had been carved by tools, not nature, and he could see the marks of axes where they'd been opened out. Some tunnels came to dead ends that looked more like rooms where people had lived and worked. But where were the people?

They'd left tools and clothing behind, even bedding, but everything was covered in a thick layer of dust. As though the people who lived here had left in a hurry, intending to return, but they had not. What had driven them out, and what had prevented them from returning? Aladdin wasn't sure he wanted to know the answer to either question.

Especially not if the answer was somewhere in the city with him. Someone or something had killed Bugra, and Aladdin had no desire to be next.

He entered, then backed out of a prayer room. Perhaps he should take a moment and pray, he thought, then decided not to bother. Who knew which direction to face, anyway, so deep underground? No one would hear his prayer from here.

The next corridor ended in a dead end, blocked off by a boulder that looked like a smaller version of the one at the entrance. A door, Aladdin guessed, eyeing it. "Please open?" he suggested.

The round stone rolled smoothly aside,

revealing a new passage. Aladdin breathed a sigh of relief, and stepped through.

More passages, more rooms, more torches, and more doors that opened at his request. Aladdin knew he descended deeper into the earth at each step, but he'd seen no sign of treasure, lamps or otherwise.

If he wanted to hide a pile of untouchable gold in this maze of a city, where would he put it? Aladdin considered this for a moment, before he had his answer. He'd put it either in the very centre of the city, or in the furthest depths from the entrance. Whichever was easier to defend if the city were attacked.

Aladdin laughed, the sound echoing through the empty tunnels. What would he know about defending or attacking a city? He should be safely home in his. All he had to do was find the benighted lamp, hand it to the madman outside, and he could go home.

Deeper he went, taking the tunnels that led down until he could go no further, for his way was barred by a bigger door than any he'd seen yet. This was the one, he was certain of it.

"Open, please," he breathed.

The door rolled open. Aladdin took a deep breath and thrust his torch inside.

At first, it didn't look too different from the store rooms he'd passed, with dusty casks, boxes and sacks piled up on either side of a narrow aisle. But something glowed at the end, as though he'd arrived at the surface and not the depths of the city.

Aladdin crept forward, suddenly glad he was so thin, for a bigger man wouldn't have fitted so easily between the chests piled up to the ceiling. The hem of his tunic dragged along the top of a chest, revealing costly polished wood under the dust. This was the treasury, all right. What had Gwandoya told him to watch out for? Not to touch the gold, or let his clothing touch it. Pulling his tunic tight around him, Aladdin proceeded forward into…the light.

The second chamber didn't look any different from the first, at first, for whoever owned the contents of this place preferred to keep it safely locked in chests, instead of piled up all over the floor, as Aladdin might have expected. Someone with countless wealth would surely be careless with their coins. But the first glimpse he got of gold was in a chest that someone had pried open so roughly it no longer closed. Bugra would not have had the strength to do this – and nor did Aladdin. How many men had Gwandoya brought here? And why had they all failed?

Aladdin rounded the corner and found his answer. A lit lamp sat in an alcove on the wall, so blackened from use it was hard to tell it was brass. But the flame was as bright as ever, illuminating a chest full of riches that surely belonged to a king or a sultan. Gold jewellery snaked around a collection of gold lamps, so shiny they hurt his eyes. Aladdin squinted, and looked again. The chest was not full – it was barely half full, and some rings and a necklace lay on the ground in front of it, as if dropped by someone in a hurry to cram as much treasure as they could into a sack to take with them.

Automatically, Aladdin stooped to return the treasures to their chest.

"I thought you were brighter than the others," a strange voice said.

Aladdin jerked upright. "Who said that?"

A blue glow appeared on Aladdin's right, atop a barrel. The light grew until it took the shape of a man. A man who was as lanky as Aladdin himself, though his clothes were far finer than anything Aladdin owned. "That would be me," the bluish man drawled, snapping his fingers. The blue light vanished, leaving the magic man looking as normal as Aladdin, or as normal as any man who hadn't appeared from a ball of light.

"Who are you?"

The man bent double without rising from the barrel. "Kaveh, servant of the ring you wear on your finger." He nodded at Aladdin's hand. "And you?

"Aladdin." He didn't know what else to say. Unemployed street rat? Minion to the madman outside? Son of a spinner? His heart lurched at the thought of what would happen to his mother if he died here. It would break her heart. "I need to grab that lamp and get it out of here." He reached for the alcove.

Kaveh whistled. "So you are brighter than the others. You're the first one who went for the right lamp."

Aladdin's hand closed around it, a moment before he realised that a lit lamp would be hot to the touch. To his surprise, the metal was as cold as the stone underfoot. "Must be magic," he muttered.

"Sure is. Why do you think that madman wants it so much?"

Aladdin hefted the lamp in his hand. It was such a small thing – his mother had two such at home, both in much better state than this. "What does it do?"

Kaveh grinned. "Give it a rub and find out."

Aladdin almost obeyed, then stopped himself. Something had killed the other men Gwandoya had sent here. He'd survived this long, but who knew what Kaveh's motives were? Perhaps he'd killed them, or tricked them into doing something that had.

"No," Aladdin said. "I have a job to do. I must fetch this lamp from the city and bring it back to Gwandoya. Then I get paid." Not enough to let him see Maram again, though, Aladdin realised with a sinking heart. A man who ate bugs wouldn't have a princess's bride price to spare. Why hadn't Aladdin thought of that before?

"The only repayment he'll give you is a slit throat. He can't risk you telling anyone what you found in here," Kaveh said, as though reading Aladdin's thoughts.

Aladdin sank onto a chest, his head in his hands. "What will I do? I have to get home. I need that money." Funny, Gwandoya had never mentioned just how much Aladdin's payment would be. Now he knew why.

"In debt, are you?"

Aladdin shook his head. "Who would lend money to someone like me? Even I know I'll never be able to repay them. No, it's…there's this girl…"

Kaveh's eyes lit up with an unearthly glow. "A girl? Is she as glorious as the moon?"

Aladdin's mind cast up a vision of Maram bathing naked in the bathhouse. The image from his dreams. "The moon herself would weep to see her, she is so beautiful."

"So you want a gift to win her affections?"

Aladdin laughed. "I would need a whole kingdom before I had a chance of that. She's the Sultan's daughter, you see, and I am no prince."

Kaveh nodded thoughtfully. "So you need a gift fit for a princess. You know, I think I can help you."

Help never came for free. "What will you want in return?" Aladdin asked.

"Don't give the madman back his ring, and I'll show you the perfect thing to win your princess's heart, and her father's, too."

Aladdin stared at Kaveh for a moment. "What do you want me to do with the ring?"

Kaveh shrugged. "Keep it. I'd like to meet this princess of yours."

"She's not mine, and she never will be," Aladdin said steadily.

Kaveh grinned. "Never say never. Women fall in love with their heart's desire, not with whoever their father wants them to marry."

Aladdin didn't bother arguing this time. Judging by his clothes, Kaveh was highborn, maybe even as highborn as Maram herself. He had no idea what it was not to be able to remember when he'd last eaten — or wonder when he might eat again.

"We'd better get this lamp up to the surface. I said I would, and my word is all I have left." Aladdin rose.

"You're a fool," Kaveh said.

Aladdin knew he was right. "Perhaps, but an honest fool."

Kaveh shook his head. "I don't have to watch this." He dissolved into sparkling blue light, which streamed into the ring before the light winked out.

Aladdin peered at his hand. It looked like an ordinary silver ring, but he knew he hadn't imagined Kaveh.

Aladdin tucked the lamp inside his tunic, before tightening his sash to make sure it didn't fall out. He'd come too far to lose it now.

The hike back through the tunnels seemed a

lot shorter now. Maybe it was because he was headed for the surface, or he knew where he was going, Aladdin wasn't sure, but there was a spring in his step as he glimpsed the yawning entrance to the cavern he'd dreaded when he first saw it. How wrong he was.

"Do you have it?" Gwandoya asked eagerly, his shadow blocking the light coming from the entrance.

Aladdin dug into his tunic and produced the sorry-looking lamp. "Yes."

Gwandoya beckoned him closer. "Give it to me!"

He wasn't just eager, he seemed…rabid, Aladdin thought uneasily.

"Where is the payment you promised me?" Aladdin demanded.

Gwandoya wet his lips. "It is back in the city. I will pay you on our return."

Back went the lamp into the depths of his clothes. "Then I will keep it a while longer."

"I said give it to me!"

His instincts screamed at him to obey, but Aladdin ignored them. "And I said pay me."

The two men stared at one another, Gwandoya's chest heaving as though it cost him a great deal not to kill Aladdin on the spot.

All the more reason to hang onto the thing the madman wanted, Aladdin told himself.

Gwandoya forced out a smile that didn't touch his eyes. "As you wish, boy. But return my ring."

"Don't do it!" Kaveh's voice whispered.

The smile died. "What did you say?"

Aladdin swallowed. "Of…of course." With shaking hands, he pulled the ring from his finger. "Come and get it."

Gwandoya's eyes blazed. "I will not set foot in that cursed city! Anyone who steals from it is turned to – "

A great rush of wind came from behind Aladdin, so powerful that it pushed the boulder door shut, leaving Gwandoya outside. The man could be heard shouting and hammering outside, but the rock didn't move.

"What in heaven's name…" Aladdin began, risking a glance over his shoulder.

"I said not to give it to him," Kaveh said calmly, pressing his back to the boulder and folding his arms.

Realisation dawned. "You opened all the doors. Even that one. No man could move that stone. Not even Gwandoya, now you're in here with me. What are you?"

"I told you. I'm the servant of the ring," Kaveh said smugly. After a moment, he relented and added, "My previous owner charged me with protecting the city. Only one who wears my ring can open the door from the outside when it is closed, and no outsider may pass through the city gates with gold from the city that does not belong to him."

Dread curdled in Aladdin's belly. "What happened to the ones who tried?"

Kaveh waved his hand behind him. "They made a generous contribution to the city's wealth."

Aladdin approached what appeared to be a line of dusty statues. He lifted his torch and reached to brush the dust off the nearest one's face.

"By all that's holy!" Aladdin jumped back. Bugra's horrified face stared back at him, above a tunic that bulged with the treasures he'd tried to steal. Too heavy for him to carry, Aladdin realised, for they'd cursed him into a gold statue. He swallowed. "What have you done to him?"

Kaveh shrugged. "My master wanted me to just kill them, but who wanted decaying corpses stinking up the city gates? Especially if no one was home. So I thought gold statues might be better. When the prince returns, he can melt them down for the treasury."

"Will that hurt them?" Aladdin asked.

"Of course not. They're dead. Does a chicken feel when you roast its corpse?"

Unbidden, Aladdin's stomach growled even louder this time. "I would much prefer a chicken to a statue," he admitted.

Kaveh clapped his hands. "I can help you there. I know where the prince's store rooms are, where he keeps a lifetime supply of honeyed dates, among other delicacies."

Though he was now trapped in an

underground city with a strange man who glowed blue, while another madman hammered on the gates, for the first time since he'd left home, Aladdin began to feel the tiniest bit better about his future. Any future that held honeyed dates had to be good, he was sure of it.

Ten

"Your Highness, the woman is here," the maid said, bowing low. There was a slight emphasis on the word 'woman' that made it sound like an insult.

Maram set down her sewing, already inclined to be grateful to Aladdin's mother. She'd never much liked sewing, but she'd needed to do something with her hands to still her impatience. Now the search was over, she could stop. "Is she alone?"

"Yes, Princess."

Maram fought to hide her disappointment. "See that she is served refreshments while she waits. I will be there directly."

Maram chose her favourite gown, a jewelled thing that impressed even the richest kings, for this audience, and struggled not to tap her foot with impatience as her maids dressed her. Her reflection was quite dazzling to behold, Maram fancied, turning this way and that in front of her mirror. Too dazzling for a woman Aladdin had described as a simple spinner?

Of course it was.

She ordered her maids to bring her the plainest gown she owned. Maram should have known better. They brought her a gown of a purple so deep, it appeared black, with a matching veil. Tiny glass beads sewn onto it only helped complete the illusion, for they were invisible against the black. To the casual observer, she appeared to be in deep mourning, but once light hit the fabric, it glimmered like the starry sky over the desert. It was far from plain, but it would have to do.

When her maids had made sure the veil

covered all but her eyes, as befitted a princess at a public audience, Maram headed out of her apartment into the palace proper.

As she approached the room where she'd asked Aladdin's mother to be shown to, she heard raised voices. No, one raised voice – a wailing woman, rising over the softer male voices in the room.

Maram's heart constricted in her chest. Had something happened to Aladdin? No, surely not. She stepped into the room, unnoticed.

A woman in black rose up onto her knees, clutching the hem of a guard's tunic in her white-knuckled hands. "Please, tell me what you have done with my son. He's a good boy, he would not do anything to offend the Sultan. Take me instead!" She collapsed on the floor, sobbing, before she accosted the other guard with a similar plea.

Neither guard seemed to know what to do with the woman, and they both looked relieved to see Maram.

"You may go," Maram said, then surveyed the room. "Where are the refreshments I asked for? See that they are brought here immediately."

"Yes, Your Highness." The two men bowed and hurried out.

The woman threw herself full length on the floor before Maram. "Your Highness, please have mercy on a poor mother. Tell me why you have imprisoned my son."

"Aladdin is in prison?"

The woman let out a wail. "It is a mistake, a misunderstanding! My son would never do anything to offend the Sultan!"

Maram shook her head. "Mistress, please, get up. Tell me what has happened to Aladdin."

The woman rose to her knees, wiping her eyes with her veil. Hers was black, though so threadbare Maram could see through it. "I do not know. He left to find work, as he does every morning, but he did not return. No one has seen him. Then some guards came to my humble house and told me to come with them to answer questions about my son. Please, Your Highness, tell me what he has done!"

Maram beckoned one of the guards back into the room. He stood in the doorway, reluctant to enter any further. "Send a man to the prisons, to see if a man named Aladdin is held there, and if he is, find out what his crime may be."

The man bowed deeply. "I will, Your Highness, but we already checked there. There is no prisoner of that name anywhere in the city. The only Aladdin we could find is reputed to be this woman's son, so we brought her. As she said, the man has not been seen for days."

Maram nodded and dismissed him. "Mistress…please, can you tell me your name?"

"This humble mother is called Sadaf, Your Highness."

"Mistress Sadaf, please, sit with me." Maram gestured to the table where – finally! – the food and drink had been laid out. She gestured for one of the maids to shut the door behind her and Maram was alone with Aladdin's mother. Only then did she unwind her veil so that Aladdin's mother might see her face.

Sadaf crept timidly to the cushion Maram indicated, still not raising her eyes to Maram's face.

Maram settled on her own cushion. "Mistress Sadaf, I have invited you here to…" What could she say? She wanted to ask where Aladdin had been since that day in the bathhouse, but if she had no idea where he was… "I wish to ask about your son," Maram said finally. "Is it possible that he has left the city?"

Sadaf shook her head. "Aladdin has never stepped out of the city gates, Your Highness. He was born here, and he has never left. So when he did not come home, I thought…" She covered her mouth, but not fast enough to hold in a sob.

"We will find him," Maram said, though she had no idea how. If her father's men hadn't found him inside the city by now, it stood to reason that he was either not in the city or he was dead. No, surely not dead.

Sadaf burst into noisy tears. "Thank you, Your Highness. I do not know what we have done to earn such kindness, but if there is anything I can do to repay you, tell me, and it is yours."

"If he returns…when he returns," Maram corrected herself, "Send him to the palace to see me."

"Who should he ask for, Your Highness? If my son came to the palace, asking to see a princess, he would surely be turned away," Sadaf said.

She was right. No one would see Aladdin the way Maram did. "Tell him to ask for Princess Maram. No, he is to tell the guards that Princess Maram commanded him to present himself at the palace." They would believe that.

"As you command, Your Highness." Sadaf bowed low.

"No, I don't. I ask…" Maram stopped, lost. "Mistress Sadaf, please understand me. It is not a command. That is only what he must tell the guards. Tell Aladdin…tell Aladdin that I wish to see him, and if he wishes to see me, what to say to the guards." There, that sounded better.

Sadaf's knowing eyes were upon her, and Maram didn't know where to look.

"My son is as charming as his father. I do not know how you came to meet him, Your Highness, but if my son is in prison, then it is because he is accused of being a thief," Sadaf said.

"Aladdin is a thief?" She didn't want to believe it. If he was a thief, surely he would have stolen something from her in the bathhouse. He hadn't touched her jewels, her clothes…nothing.

Sadaf smiled faintly. "My son has never stolen anything in his life, or so I had thought, but a princess's heart is something so precious, so priceless, perhaps he could not resist." She bowed low once more. "I will do as you ask, Your Highness, if I am lucky enough to see my son alive again."

Without waiting to be dismissed, Sadaf backed out of the room, and left.

Maram couldn't seem to close her mouth. Were her feelings for Aladdin that obvious?

Surely she did not look as hopelessly enamoured of him as the royalty of the northern lands were of her. Surely not.

She shook the silly thought out of her head. What she looked like and what Sadaf thought didn't matter. Aladdin was missing, and if he'd been missing long enough for his mother to despair of his return…he must be found.

Eleven

Aladdin woke to find his head pounding, as though he'd drunk too much wine. As if he could afford to drink wine. "Where in heaven's name am I?" he asked the inky darkness.

"Tasnim, the forgotten city," a familiar voice replied, as a glimmering blue ball appeared and expanded to become a man. Kaveh.

"And why does it feel like a camel stomped on my head?"

"That would be the cask of Prince Firdaus' private reserve you drank." Kavek sounded amused. "It's powerful stuff, or it was a century ago, when he first bought it. Now it must be strong enough to kill an ox. I told you to drink sparingly, but you told me you were too thirsty."

Aladdin lurched to his feet. "Well, now I don't want wine. I want water. I'm sure I saw a well around here somewhere."

"You won't find any water in it. Why do you think all the people left? Without water, the city would die."

Kaveh began to tell a story about a ruling prince who vanished when the water did, and the fate of his people, but Aladdin shut him out and concentrated on looking for water. His mouth tasted like rats had nested in it and used his throat for a privy. He never wanted to drink wine again.

In the faint blue light from Kaveh following him, Aladdin came to one of the wells he remembered. A dusty bucket lay on the ground beside the well, so he hooked it up to the rope and lowered it into the depths, praying for the splash.

He'd almost lost hope when he heard it — though the sound was faint and deep. Aladdin let the bucket drop lower, then began hauling it up again, hand over hand. It was heavier than before, he was certain of it.

When the bucket rose into sight, the blue reflection on the surface of the liquid of the brimming pail was enough for him to let out a hoarse cheer.

"I wouldn't drink that if I were you," Kaveh said.

Aladdin ignored him again. He lifted the bucket to his lips and only then did the stench reach him. Aladdin coughed. "What is that? It can't be water."

Kaveh grinned. "Well, it was once water. Before some bastard pissed it out, maybe, and threw it down the well before he left the city. Where it's been festering ever since."

Aladdin gagged and tipped the bucket's contents back where they'd come from. "Is there no water in the city at all?"

Kaveh shook his head. "That's what I've been trying to tell you. There's no water here.

The only liquid to drink in this city is wine."

Aladdin had drunk enough wine to last him a lifetime. "So where's the nearest source of water?"

"Half a day's ride, back the way we came."

Of course it was. The oasis where Gwandoya had first called a halt, Aladdin would wager.

"How long would it take to walk?"

Kaveh eyed him critically. "Forever. You wouldn't last the distance, not as starved as you are. You'd need to stay here for a month at least, emptying the royal larders, before you had sufficient strength."

"There isn't enough water here to last a month."

Kaveh brightened. "But there is more than enough wine, even after seeing the way you drink it. You'll need a flask or two for the journey, for it is at least a full night's march to the oasis."

"A month? My mother will go mad with worry over me. I must set out as soon as night falls."

Kaveh shook his head. "And I thought you were a bright one. You will not survive, you fool. And what of the treasure you wanted to take back to win your princess? Even if you had the strength to make it to the oasis before the sun rises, you would not be able to carry anything of value back with you. If you return home, it will be poorer than when you left."

The princess? Maram was the least of Aladdin's concerns now. But taking something home as payment seemed like a good idea. At least he'd have something to show for this foolishness. "What of the curse that prevents thieves leaving with their ill-gotten goods?" Aladdin asked suspiciously. "Are you trying to get me turned into a statue like the others, so that I can enrich the city, too?"

"I'll carry it out," Kaveh said. "The curse doesn't apply to me. Why, I could proclaim you as the new Prince of Tasnim, rightful owner of the city and all its riches, and no one would contradict me!"

"A prince?" Aladdin tried to sound sceptical, but the tantalising thought of walking into the

Sultan's palace, being announced as a prince, before asking for Maram's hand in marriage, was too strong to resist.

Kaveh smiled. "A fitting husband for a princess, if you carry a suitable gift for her and for her father."

For even just the chance of seeing Maram again, it was worth the risk. "A week, then. In seven days, when the sun sets, I will set out for the oasis."

"And while we wait, I shall show you all the secrets of Tasnim, and its treasures." Kaveh's grin broadened. "Treasures fit for a princess, as you shall see. What the prince kept in his harem was vastly superior to what he locked in his treasury."

"I thought you said everyone was gone. Do you mean to say the women are still here?" Aladdin asked, horrified. "We have to save them!"

"The prince's concubines were the first to leave, taking all their jewels with them. I am sure they are as far from the city as they can get." Kaveh's eyes glowed brighter. "No, it is what they did not take that I must show you."

Aladdin nodded. "Then let me find a flagon of wine, if there is nothing else to drink in this place, so that I may break my fast and drink to the vanished prince's health, before I steal his most precious treasures." This did not sit well with Aladdin, but what other choice did he have?

"As the Prince of Tasnim, you cannot steal your own things. They are yours, as is everything in the city. You shall see." Kaveh said. "I have proclaimed it, therefore it must be so!"

Aladdin sighed. He'd gone from one madman's clutches to another, and still he had none of the promised wealth either had lured him with. Oh, he still had the blackened lamp, tucked into his tunic, but what use was such a thing here? Still, this madman had the only light in the city, and he was the only man who could open the doors, so Aladdin followed him deeper into the labyrinth. It seemed the most sensible thing to do.

For the moment.

Twelve

Kaveh pushed open the city gates, then peered outside. "There's no one here," he reported. "Just like I told you."

Aladdin breathed out a sigh of relief. If Gwandoya wasn't waiting for him, then perhaps he would be able to make it home alive. He still had a desert to cross, a daunting thought even with Kaveh's help.

"Do you have the wineskins?" Aladdin asked. He would drink the contents tonight, and refill them with water when they reached the oasis. After he had drunk his fill of water for the first time in a week.

"I have the wineskins, and everything else you wanted. I may not be a particularly powerful djinn, but I do have some talents," Kaveh said with a sniff.

Talents such as carrying enormously heavy loads, or moving heavy things, Aladdin knew now. And to be visible or not, as he chose, along with whatever he was touching. A week with the man had given him a greater understanding of both Kaveh and the city of Tasnim. But there was still one question he hadn't answered…

"Why are you helping me again?" Aladdin asked.

"To see this princess of yours," Kaveh replied. "I told you that."

Aladdin sighed. Kaveh could keep his secrets. Aladdin had enough to worry about. "Let's go, then, or we will never reach the city where she lives."

The sun might have sunk behind the desert dunes, but the sand still held its heat, which bit at Aladdin's boots. Boots Kaveh had insisted he take from the prince's things, along with suitable clothing for braving the desert. So now Aladdin wore fabric finer than even Kaveh, and leather so soft he wanted to stroke it. So if he died in the desert, at least his corpse would be well-dressed, Aladdin consoled himself, then snorted. Small consolation for failure. He did not intend to fail. He intended to live, and return home to his mother, and maybe, just maybe, see Maram again.

It was hope that kept him trudging through the desert dunes until the sun rose high in the sky, following Kaveh's directions even as the heat shimmered off the sand and blinded him. Every valley seemed an oasis, but when he reached it, there was no water to be found.

It was nearly noon when Aladdin reached the oasis, and he threw himself face down in the water, gulping his fill. He would have drowned there, perhaps, if not for Kaveh, who dragged him into the shade formed by a stand of palm trees. Aladdin fell into an uneasy doze, which turned into sleep as the sun sank once more.

Kaveh woke him at dawn. "Time to move, or you will be roasted alive," he said.

Aladdin managed to make it to the makeshift shelter Kaveh had constructed while he slept. Fallen palm fronds and some coarse sacking made a bower out of the hastily dug hole in the ground, but Aladdin was nevertheless grateful for it. Kaveh produced some nuts – Aladdin didn't dare ask where from – and a filled water skin, then told Aladdin to rest.

Despite spending all night asleep, Aladdin had no trouble obeying the djinn. He'd never walked so far in his life, and as soon as night fell, he had the other half of his journey to finish. If he survived the day.

To Aladdin's surprise, Kaveh woke him at sunset, and he almost felt optimistic about his chances of reaching home.

The oasis was scarcely out of sight by the time Aladdin disabused himself of that notion. The blisters he'd barely noticed on the first day had swelled to carbuncles in his boots, and the sun had found him inside his little shelter while he slept, burning his skin as surely as boiling water would. Yet on he slogged, for Aladdin knew he was headed home.

One foot in front of the other, until he could go no further. Aladdin fell to his knees. "I can't," he wheezed.

"I'm not going to let you die out here, so some corpse robber can pick me up. Get up!" Kaveh slid an arm under Aladdin's shoulders and heaved him to his feet. "If I have to carry you the rest of the way, we're going to reach the city!"

So Aladdin staggered on, while Kaveh helped him, until Aladdin saw what looked like the city gates looming before him, lit with the fierce light of a desert dawn. "I'm home," Aladdin mumbled.

"Not yet you're not. Where do you live?" Kaveh asked grimly, his grip tightening around Aladdin.

Aladdin pointed and mumbled something he hoped made sense. He was moving again, so Kaveh must have understood some of it, at least.

"Do you recognise this place?" Kaveh asked impatiently.

Aladdin peered blearily at the worn door he'd opened and closed a thousand times. "Home."

"Good." Kaveh shoved the door open.

Aladdin staggered inside, then pitched forward into oblivion.

Kaveh cursed. "Hello, lady of the house! Is this your son?" he called.

A woman emerged from the dimness, hastily wrapping a veil around her hair. "I…Aladdin?"

Aladdin was beyond responding.

"I found him outside the city walls," Kaveh said. "He said he lived here."

"He does! Oh, how can I ever thank you? Or repay you?" the woman asked, falling to her knees beside Aladdin. "You have answered a mother's prayer."

Kaveh smiled. "Granting wishes, who'd have thought?" While Aladdin's mother was distracted, Kaveh disappeared. For the moment, his job was done.

Thirteen

"Have you heard anything?" Maram asked fretfully.

The guardsman shook his head. "No, Your Highness. I have told the prison guards to send word if they see a man with that name but no one has seen him. Are you sure he exists?"

"Of course he does! And so does his mother!" Maram snapped.

The guard bowed deeply. "My apologies, Princess, if I have offended you."

If this man knew half the things she'd seen and done in foreign courts, he would not worry about offending her. Maram hid her smile. "You are forgiven. I am…frustrated. I do not understand how a man can vanish in this city and not be found."

"Perhaps he is not in the city, Your Highness."

She'd thought the same thing, but Sadaf had insisted Aladdin never left the city. Sadaf…perhaps she should send for the woman again?

Maram considered for a moment, then shook her head. No, Sadaf had promised to send word if her son returned. If she had half the honour of her son, then she would notify the palace the instant Aladdin returned.

Unless he did not want to see her…

Maram swallowed. If Aladdin did not want to see her again, would Sadaf tell her? Or would she worry about offending a princess, too?

"If you have not heard anything by the end of the week, summon Sadaf the spinner to the palace," Maram said.

Another bow. "As you wish, Your Highness."

No, what she wished was to see Aladdin now, at this very moment, but Maram knew as well as anyone that wishes were seldom granted, and when they were, they would rarely be what one wants.

So she sighed and forced herself to find some distraction to keep her mind busy until she received the word she wanted, or the week ended. Whatever came first.

Fourteen

Aladdin was certain he had to be dreaming, for he distinctly heard his mother's voice, and his mother never left the city. Even if Berk had told her where her son had gone, there was no way she would venture out alone to search for him, and she did not have the money to hire men to help her.

So he took his time opening his eyes, for surely he had collapsed in the desert, and the sun above would be drinking the last drops of water from his body before it killed him. At least the last thing he heard would be his mother's voice and not Gwandoya's mad laughter. And dying of thirst was faster, kinder than a slow death by starvation. He almost felt like he was lying on a bed, instead of in the unforgiving sand. Still, the sand at the oasis had been soft…

But someone would find his body, and the ring, and Kaveh would be angry that some corpse robber had him. So Aladdin had to get up, and struggle on, or Kaveh would roll a boulder across him…

Aladdin forced his eyes open and sat up. His head hurt like he'd drunk too much wine again, but he'd grown used to that in Tasnim. He blinked away the blurriness, waiting to see either the desert or the rock walls of Tasnim. What he did not expect to see were the whitewashed walls of his mother's house.

"Maman?" he croaked. If this truly was her house, she must be here, for he'd heard her voice.

He heard something crash to the floor. "Aladdin?" A moment later, she emerged from the gloom.

"How did I get here?" he asked. "And do you have any water?"

"Of course!" She reached down and only now did Aladdin see the jug and cup on the floor beside him. She filled the cup and handed it to him.

Aladdin drained it, then refilled it himself and drank a second cup before his parched throat felt moistened enough to speak. "How did I get here?"

Maman shot a dark glance over her shoulder. "Your friend, Kaveh, carried you in here, half dead from exposure and thirst. He comes every day, bringing food and other things, but he refuses to take any money or thanks for it. And he disappears, like he has done again. It is as though he does not wish to be seen here."

Something tightened around Aladdin's finger, before the pressure eased as quickly as it had come. Kaveh's ring. He was not gone, the pressure reminded him.

"I will settle everything with him, Maman,"

Aladdin promised. "You don't need to worry about it."

"I do not trust him. Yes, he saved your life, but he has secrets that he does not say." His mother frowned.

"Let the man keep his secrets. He is allowed to them."

"We still must pay him. Did you bring any money back from whatever you were doing? I searched your clothes, but all I found was this thing." She held up the blackened lamp. "Perhaps we can get a coin or two for it. It is heavy brass. If I can polish it well, perhaps enough to pay him back a small amount…"

Before Aladdin could stop her, she spat on the lamp and began to rub at it furiously with a handful of her skirt.

Blue smoke erupted from the spout of the lamp, pouring out until it filled the room from floor to ceiling. Just like with the ring, the smoke took the form of a man, a man so enormous he had to bend double to fit in the room.

"I am the servant of the lamp," the smoky

man boomed. "What do you wish of me?"

Maman's eyes widened in terror, and she whimpered as she tried to back away from the djinn, for surely this was another of Kaveh's kind. Then she overbalanced, falling backward and striking her head against the wall.

"Maman! Are you all right?" Aladdin asked, rushing to check. The back of her head was bleeding from where it had hit the wall, but she still drew breath. He carried her to the bed, not sure what else to do.

"I said: what do you wish of me?"

Aladdin whirled to face the djinn. The lamp had fallen to the floor, so he picked it up. "You frightened my mother and now she is hurt. I wish you would fix the mess you have made."

"I cannot undo what has been done, but I can heal her," the djinn said.

Aladdin blinked in surprise. It took him a moment before he had the presence of mind to say, "Then do it."

He watched in fascination as the djinn bent over his mother, holding out his hands. Blue light arced from his hands to her, until her head was enveloped in a blue cloud. Then he waved his hand and the light died. "It is done," the djinn said. "When she wakes, it will be as though she was never injured. What else do you wish of me?"

Aladdin wet his lips. "Answers. What are you?"

"I am the servant of the lamp, and my master is whoever holds it in his hands."

"So you are a djinn?"

"Yes."

"You can perform magic? What sort of magic can you do?"

The djinn swelled to fill half the room. "I can make you the richest man alive. Transport you to the farthest reaches of the Earth and back again in the blink of an eye. Build you a palace so magnificent even the Sultan will beg to see inside."

Aladdin sucked in a breath. He wanted all of those things, but he knew nothing came without a cost. Before he wished for anything, he needed to talk to Kaveh. He knew Kaveh, whereas this djinn was a stranger.

"What would you wish me to do first, master?" the genie rumbled.

Aladdin thought for a moment. His belly rumbled, reminding him that it had been a long time since he'd eaten. Kaveh had provided him with food, and there had been no ill consequences from that. Finally, he said, "I am hungry. Bring me something to eat."

The djinn bowed low, then vanished.

"Show off," Kaveh muttered, emerging like a wraith from the ring. "Mister high and mighty, all powerful master of everything."

"Do you know him?"

Kaveh glared at the lamp. "I have seen him before, yes. Prince Philemon was master of the lamp for a time, before he disappeared, and he had no need for me when he had him. He handed me to one of his servants, who sold me to buy bread after he left the city. To the madman I'd rather not return to."

"Would you rather I'd asked you to fetch my food?"

Kaveh looked affronted. "You had no need

to ask him for anything. I gave you the contents of the royal larder! I still have some of it, too. If I can remember where I hid it. Must be here somewhere, the house isn't that big…" He wandered about the room, waving his arms as though he expected to touch something unseen. "Ah, here! You liked the prince's almonds, so I brought two barrels."

"I liked them because they were the only thing that didn't require cooking, or taste so sweet they made me terribly thirsty," Aladdin replied. He'd eaten so many almonds in the last week, he'd happily live the rest of his life without eating another.

"Oh," Kaveh seemed crestfallen, but not for long. "I brought the prince's garden, too. That will impress your princess, you'll see."

"The entire garden?" Aladdin had briefly wandered through what Kaveh had called the harem gardens, a large, high-ceilinged cavern filled with artificial trees made of metal and gemstones. Every jewelled leaf, flower and fruit had been lovingly crafted so each was unique, but under all the dust Aladdin had found it hard to be impressed. It had looked so forlorn, a world that had once glittered with magic but was now brown and dull with dust.

"Just the trees. Most of the shrubs. And all the flowers."

The entire garden, then.

"Where did you put it all?"

Kaveh opened his mouth. "Ah – "

A cloud of blue smoke exploded into the room, then parted to reveal a host of golden dishes bearing a banquet of more food than Aladdin had ever seen in his life. Things that could only have come from the palace kitchen, or one like it.

"Your meal, master," the huge djinn boomed.

Maman screwed up her face, moving restlessly in the bed as though she were about to wake. She would not be happy to see the giant djinn in the house still.

"Now, go hide in the lamp, or wherever it is you go, until I summon you again," Aladdin said.

The djinn set the dishes down and

disappeared.

Just in time, for Maman sat up. "What was that thing?"

"Nothing, Maman. I have food for us. What would you like to eat?"

Maman looked around in bewilderment. "Where did you get the money for so much food, or such dishes?"

Kaveh had disappeared again, leaving Aladdin to explain on his own. "I fear you would not believe me, Maman. It is a story for another time. But I did not steal them, and they belong to us now. Of that I am certain. Now, let us eat, and when we are done, perhaps we can sell the dishes to a goldsmith so we can buy you some new clothes."

Maman nodded. "Very well. We can talk after we have eaten."

For the first time in longer than he could remember, Aladdin sat down to a meal with his mother, where they both ate their fill. For once, he'd done something right.

Fifteen

"You wished to see me, Father?" Maram asked as she stepped into the Sultan's lavish apartments. She did not want to go on another diplomatic mission until she knew what had happened to Aladdin, but she could hardly refuse. "Which part of the world would you like me to conquer next?"

He laughed, for he knew as well as Maram did that she spoke only partly in jest. "No, I am happy to have you home, daughter, at least for now. It is your future I am thinking of, and all the conquests you have already made. You deserve a reward."

Maram clapped her hands. "Then you will build a bigger bathhouse on the palace grounds? I know just the place…"

Father shook his head. "No, we have all the bathhouses we need. And you will not be here to use it when it is built, so where would the point be in that?"

Maram's heart turned cold. "Where will I be, Father?" This news did not bode well.

He waved for her to sit down. Maram selected a fat cushion and took her seat.

"You know that my Vizier, Ali, has been a good and faithful adviser to me since I ascended to my father's throne. As deserving of reward as you, in fact," the Sultan began.

Maram nodded slowly. Yes, Ali was a good adviser to her father. He had an astute mind and while she did not always agree with him on international relations, she still respected his experience in matters of local politics. "He has had several wives, and many children by them. A new, young wife would be a burden to him,

I am sure."

"Indeed, and so he has told me. In fact, when I asked him what reward he would want from me in return for his loyal service, his thoughts were for his children."

Maram waited, her dread building. She had no intention of training some poor girl to be a courtesan. She might have chosen this path for herself, but she would not recommend it for anyone, and she would fight her father if he tried to force one of the Vizier's daughters to become her replacement.

"His oldest son, Hasan, who he hopes will succeed him as Vizier one day, has never married. Ali says it is because he wishes to have only one wife, the most perfect of all. It seems he has been madly in love with you since your first diplomatic mission together." Father smiled indulgently.

"Hasan can go fuck a camel, for I'll never let him touch me," Maram wanted to say, but those were not the right words to say to the Sultan. They weren't entirely true, either. She'd prefer the camel to do the fucking, forcing itself on Hasan as the man had tried to do to her.

"Hasan is not the husband I would have chosen," Maram said instead. It would be a good match for him, and also a politically astute one for her, as she and her children would never have a strong claim on the throne, so Hasan could not usurp the place of her father or, upon his death, one of her brothers.

"I had not thought to ask you to choose a husband yet, but Anahita tells me it is time," Father continued.

Maram's blood boiled. Why, that little sneak. Avenging herself on Maram for suggesting Anahita marry again. If Anahita hadn't already left the palace to seek her new husband, Maram would slap her silly. She still would, when she saw Anahita again, for the girl never stayed married for long.

Maram forced herself to swallow down her ire. She was a politician, she knew how to negotiate better than anyone. "Perhaps it is time for me to marry, before I am too old for motherhood. But I would not want to marry a man who is unworthy, or who could not provide for me and my children. I am comfortable here in the palace, Father, and I would not wish to live anywhere less comfortable. Before I consent to marry this man, I would like to see him build me a palace fit for a princess." With a bathhouse, she thought but did not say. Because when he failed to include a bathhouse that pleased her, she could delay further by insisting that it be built.

Father nodded thoughtfully. "Yes, you are right. He must have a house deserving of his bride. So we will announce your engagement tomorrow, as I had planned, but the wedding must wait until Hasan has provided a suitable place for you to live."

Maram allowed herself to breathe again. Construction was slow, so she would have time to locate Aladdin in that time. Perhaps even persuade him to change his mind about becoming her lover.

In the meantime, she had to find a way to stop this marriage to horrible Hasan. She should have shoved a knife in his guts when she'd had the chance, all those years ago, instead of holding it to his manhood and threatening to amputate his crown jewels if he did not leave her alone. Now…if all else failed, she would find an assassin to do the job for her.

Sixteen

"And so, that is where I have been. Exploring an underground city, getting left behind, and having to trek through the desert to get home," Aladdin finished. He'd managed to tell his mother the truth without mentioning djinn once.

"A truly alarming tale, my son. But what does this have to do with the princess?" Maman asked gravely.

Aladdin choked on his water, briefly becoming a fountain before his coughing fit eased. "What princess?"

"Her Highness Princess Maram, who summoned me to the palace to give you a message," Maman said.

"What message?" he asked faintly.

Maman scrutinised his face. "You do not seem surprised that one of the Sultan's daughters would summon me, or leave a message for you."

Now he'd done it. "I met her once in the marketplace. She was very gracious."

"What was a princess doing in the bazaar?"

He could answer this without incriminating himself too much. "She had just returned from a long journey abroad, and she was on her way to the bathhouse."

"Princesses do not..." Maman's eyes widened. "Most princesses do not. Only one does. The Traitor Queen's daughter, the witch the Sultan sends abroad to enchant foreign princes." Maman shook her head. "No wonder she is so beautiful and yet unmarried. What man would want a wife who has known more men than she can count — and foreigners, at that? Unwashed, uncouth, unmannered, with no idea of proper behaviour…and they eat the strangest things!"

No stranger than Gwandoya, though he was a foreigner, too, from southern lands instead of those in the north from whence the crusaders came. But Aladdin didn't want to think about the madman. His thoughts were of Maram, and his mother's slight to the lovely woman.

"What man would deserve her," he corrected. "Beautiful, enchanting, gracious, and the Sultan's daughter. Every man desires her, whether she wills it or no. But it is her father who will not allow her to marry. She is too valuable as an envoy to ever be free."

"Careful, my son. It sounds like you are under her spell, too. If she is forbidden to marry as you say, then you risk heartbreak even thinking about her. Forget her."

Aladdin shook his head. "I cannot. And if she gave you a message for me, then she has not forgotten me, either. Maman, please tell me…what did Princess Maram say?"

She sighed. "She wanted me to tell you to present yourself at the palace, saying she commanded you to do so. But I fear that if you do, it will only result in your doom. If you are lucky, the palace guards will turn you away. If you are not lucky…it is only a matter of time before the princess tires of you, and she will have you killed or imprisoned without hesitation. Please, I beg you, do not do as she asks."

Aladdin nodded slowly. "You are wiser than you know, Maman. The palace guards will never admit a street rat into the Sultan's palace. But you have been allowed in. You have dined with the princess herself. You must go to the palace, and present a gift to the Sultan for me. If he likes my gift, then you will ask the Sultan to summon me, so that I might beg for the hand of his daughter."

"No, I cannot. The Sultan will not see me…and what gift can you possibly offer that he will accept?"

Aladdin held out a cloth-shrouded bundle, peeling the layers away to reveal the treasure beneath. A small, jewelled shrub, perhaps two handspans in diameter, glittered in the lamplight. Each berry was made up of a cluster of amethysts so dark they almost seemed black, a stark contrast to the mother-of-pearl petalled blossoms. Together with the green agate leaves, the whole thing weighed far more than a shrub should, but Aladdin thought his mother could manage it. "Give this to the Sultan as my gift, and tell him that if he allows me to make Princess Maram my bride, I will give him a whole garden of trees and bushes such as this."

"I will take it to the Sultan, and we shall see what he says," she said doubtfully. "As long as you are sure this is what you want."

Aladdin laughed. "Maman, I have never been so sure of anything. This will work. I am certain of it."

Seventeen

Father had assembled what looked like his entire court, Maram reflected as she surveyed the crowded audience chamber. Ali the Vizier and horrible Hasan stood triumphantly on the dais at what would be her father's right hand, which was why she stood as far to the left as she could. But she wasn't hiding – even if she could in such a garish dress. The rose coloured gown and matching veil were richly embroidered in silver and gold. A diamond necklace matched the jewelled fillet that held her veil in place. Despite their magnificence, her diamonds were a calculated insult. She'd inherited them from her mother and they were well known, for the former Sultana had worn them to court as often as she attended.

Maram felt Hasan's eyes on her as her father's herald announced the Sultan's arrival.

Her father had a smile for her that she happily returned. Never mind that he wanted her to marry the wrong man – he had her happiness in mind, however misplaced his plans for it might be. No matter. Maram would make plans of her own.

The Sultan reached the dais and commanded the court to rise. This took a moment, as many had prostrated themselves and clothing had to be straightened. When the susurrus of silk-smoothing had died down, Father cleared his throat. "My subjects, before I hear today's petitions, I have happy news to share with you. My daughter, Princess Maram, is engaged to marry Vizier Ali's son, Hasan. The wedding will take place once Hasan has finished building a palace suitable to house my favourite daughter."

Hasan's grin died as he stared at the Sultan in horror. Ah, Father had not warned him earlier, it seemed. Maram made no effort to hide her triumphant smile as she surveyed the cheering crowd. A royal wedding meant a feast, and an excuse to show off their finery, with perhaps the opportunity to win favours from the celebrating Sultan or the newlyweds.

Only one pair of eyes appeared as shocked as Hasan's – that of Aladdin's mother, Sadaf. She stood at the back of the crowd, barely visible behind the more pushy petitioners, but she met Maram's gaze as squarely as though the two women were equals, so great was her shock.

When the cheering died down, Maram excused herself and made her way through the crowd to where she'd seen Sadaf. She needed to speak to the woman, to ask if her son had returned.

Yet when she reached the back of the audience chamber, Sadaf was nowhere in sight. Maram hurried outside, hoping to catch the woman before she left.

"You arrogant bitch. When you are my wife, I will see that you learn your place," a voice behind her snarled.

Ah, Hasan. He'd followed her out here.

"If I become your wife. You forget you have a palace to build first," Maram returned. There were a dozen guardsmen within hearing distance – if Hasan so much as touched her, they would arrest him in an instant at her command. But if she married him…he'd probably try to beat her to death. Try, and succeed.

"I'll build a brothel for the likes of you. That should be good enough for the whore to foreign pigs."

More than ever, Maram regretted letting this man live. Not for long. She'd find an assassin before sunset.

Maram smiled sweetly. "Build as many brothels as you wish. I'm sure you will need all the money you can muster to build a palace that meets my expectations. Oh, did my father not tell you? When he said you must build a palace fit for a princess, it is this very princess who will judge its quality. My place will be a palace as befits my high station. Whether it is my father's palace or yours will be up to you." She scanned the square, but it seemed that Sadaf had disappeared.

Cursing Hasan for distracting her, she headed back to her apartments. Her only consolation was that she left him cursing just as colourfully behind her.

<h1 style="text-align:center">Eighteen</h1>

Aladdin didn't bother to greet his mother when she returned. "What did the Sultan say?" he asked eagerly.

Maman set her cloth-wrapped bundle down. "The Sultan said the princess is to marry the Vizier's son, and he is building a magnificent palace for her. You are too late, my son. I told you she would only bring hurt and heartbreak."

A magnificent palace…where had Aladdin heard those words before? Not from his mother, surely.

It wasn't until he sat down to the noon meal with his mother, the remains of the royal repast the djinn had brought for them the previous night, that he remembered it was the djinn who'd mentioned palaces. And how he could build them.

"Maman, I need you to go back to court, and speak to the Sultan."

She stared at him. "Did you not hear what I said? She is marrying someone else, as soon as the palace is finished! Did you lose your wits out in the desert, and bring back madness in its place?"

Aladdin laughed. He did feel a little giddy, but only because he could feel happiness in his grasp. Maram had a chance at freedom – marriage to the Vizier's son would grant her that. All she needed was a suitable palace – a palace he now had the power to provide, thanks to Gwandoya. "No, Maman. I brought something far more valuable with me. Do you recall the lamp you tried to clean last night? It is no ordinary lamp. It contains a djinn."

She shuddered. "Djinn are unholy creatures, traitorous magicians who deserved to die for their crimes, but the sultan they pretended to serve was merciful and let them live on in slavery instead. If that lamp contains a djinn, you had better throw it into a deep well, where it can no longer harm you. I shall do it myself." She rose and looked about her.

Aladdin was doubly glad he'd hidden the lamp. "No, Maman. I shall deal with the lamp. I need you to speak to the Sultan. Do you still have the gift?"

Maman waved irritably at the bundle. "I wish I did not, for it is a cumbersome thing."

"Give it to the Sultan, as I asked you to this morning. Beg him to grant me a private audience tomorrow morning, when I will bring another gift, more sizeable than the first." Silently, he prayed that the djinn had not lied about his abilities. If he had, then at least Aladdin would have the garden. That was something, at least.

Maman pushed her dish away. "I am no longer hungry. I will go now, for the sooner we put an end to this folly, the better. I ask only one thing. If the Sultan refuses to see you, will you forget about the princess, and pursue more sensible things? There are plenty of merchants' daughters in the city who would happily agree to marry a handsome boy like you. I would like grandchildren."

No merchant's daughter would spare him a second glance, Aladdin knew, and nor should any princess, either. If the Sultan did grant him an audience, Aladdin would need to dress like he belonged in the palace. More to ask for. He hoped it would not be too much.

His mother departed for the palace, grumbling as long as she was in sight.

Aladdin slipped back into the house and shut the door. "Kaveh, is my mother correct? Are all djinn evil?"

Kaveh burst from the ring in a flash of blinding blue light. "What have I ever done to you that you call me evil?" he demanded.

Aladdin cast his mind back, trying to recall his mother's exact words. "Maybe not evil. Just traitorous. Are you a traitor?"

Kaveh's dark eyes burned. "There was once a sultan who called me that. Now he was evil, in the worst sense of the word. Half the kingdom wanted him dead, me included. I led the rebellion that brought the palace down on his head, crushing him beneath the stone. His successor, a man who had fanned the flames of our rebellion to white-hot heat, only to reap more benefits from it than anyone else, was my judge. He could not risk another rebellion, he said, so all traitors must be punished. Many of my men were executed, and my family had perished at the old sultan's hands, so I stood alone, the last of all of them. I expected death, but he saw fit to grant me life. A lifetime of servitude, as a servant to the ring, a punishment reserved for magic-wielders who betray their rulers. I believe he meant it as a gift to me, but a warning to everyone else that he would not tolerate treachery, for I had pledged my loyalty to the Sultan before him."

"Who or what do you serve?"

Kaveh let out a weary sigh. "I am the servant of the ring you wear, remember? As long as you wear it, I serve you."

"At what cost to me?"

A new respect dawned in Kaveh's eyes. "You must wear it always, for I will pass to the ring's new owner should you lose it. But other than that…no, I bear the cost of my servitude. The spells I cast come from the magic in my blood, blood I am bound to shed in your service and anyone else who wears the ring."

"What about the djinn of the lamp?"

Kaveh shrugged. "He is bound as I am. If you wish to know his crimes, you must ask him, for I do not know. Both of us are bound to use our magic to serve our masters, and perform whatever magic they wish of us, if we can."

"What can you do?"

"I can move things with magic, or make things unseen. I could carry you through the desert, if you commanded it, or make you invisible, but if you were to ask me to enchant this princess so that she falls deeply in love with you, that is something I cannot do. I have no aptitude for seduction magic."

"And the other djinn?"

Kaveh glared at something over Aladdin's shoulder. "Why don't you ask him? He's been listening to every word we say, but only now does he make an appearance. You should probably consider yourself honoured, for his previous master had to polish his lamp before he'd deign to help him, and even then, his gifts were tainted."

Aladdin turned, and found the second djinn standing behind him. He still towered over them both, but he evidently didn't feel the need to be as impressive as he had yesterday. Did Aladdin imagine it, or was there some sadness behind the djinn's otherwise impassive expression?

"Servant of the lamp, you said you can build me a palace. In the blink of an eye, you said. Is it true?" Aladdin demanded.

"I did not. A palace I can build, but it will take at least a night to truly be worthy of being called a palace."

Aladdin nodded. "Then I wish you to build a palace beside the one where the Sultan resides, yet more magnificent than the Sultan's. It must have…it must have…" He struggled to think of anything he knew a palace should have. He'd never been inside one before. "A bathhouse befitting a princess. Like the ancient one near the city gates. So that Princess Maram may bathe whenever she wishes without having to leave home."

The djinn's eyes widened. "The palace is not for you?"

"I wish that it could be, but no. This palace will be my gift to Princess Maram, to celebrate her marriage."

The djinn bowed low. "It shall be done, master. By dawn, you shall have your palace." He vanished.

"If I didn't know better, I'd say the man is half in love with your princess, too," Kaveh said. "He had a strange look in his eye. I wouldn't trust him if I were you."

"Says one traitor of another," Aladdin returned. Too hastily, perhaps, for he agreed with Kaveh. The nameless djinn had many secrets he had not yet shared to be trusted fully yet, if ever.

Kaveh bowed his head. "I betrayed an evil man, and I do not regret it. I would do it again. But I have served many sultans and princes since, and I have never been tempted to turn traitor again. Sometimes a man must break his own vows to do what is honourable. But the servant of the lamp…I do not know his crime, or who he betrayed. Some traitors dishonour their liege with every breath."

Aladdin nodded. Sage words from a man who by the sound of things had lived far longer than a normal man. Tomorrow, he would have his answer. But in the meantime…

"Can you make sure the palace includes a place for your garden? I would like to see it in all its glory, laid out for the princess."

Kaveh bowed and attempted to imitate the other djinn's tone: "It shall be done, master." He laughed. "Those jewels never looked right underground. By the time I am done, your garden shall sparkle in the sun like the treasure it is. You deserve it, and this princess, too."

Aladdin wanted to believe him, but he didn't

dare. Not yet.

Nineteen

"The Sultan, Your Highness," a maid announced.

Maram dropped her embroidery and rose to her feet. "Father. What an unexpected surprise."

He smiled. "I have something that will surprise even you, I think, for I find it so unbelievable I must show you to be certain I have not imagined it all." He pulled off his jewelled turban and scratched his head, a sure sign that this was no official visit.

Maram ordered refreshments and settled her father in the place of honour before taking her place across from him. "I feel like a child, waiting for a bedtime story," she admitted. "Will you tell your tale, Father?"

He sipped from his cup, then set it down. "I hardly know where to begin. After you left this morning, I held my usual audience. The petitions were so dull I found myself falling into a doze. If it weren't for Ali at my side, I suspect I might have snored. But he is a loyal vizier who would never let me do such a thing. An hour ago, I decided I wanted to retire, and opened my mouth to say so. Yet as I raised my eyes, they met the gaze of a woman who refused to look away. I fancied those dark eyes seemed to accuse me of something, though I knew not what. Instead of signalling an end to the audience, I told Ali I would see one last petitioner – her.

"When the guards brought her forward, at first, I thought they were mistaken. She threw herself face down before the dais, barely daring to say a word for some time. Long enough for me to see she wore mourning black, but both her veil and gown were so well-worn it had faded to grey. Cheap stuff, too, like she was one of the poorest in the city. What could one such as her wish to accuse me of? Curiosity baited me, so I commanded her to speak."

Father drained his cup and indicated he wanted it refilled.

"She raised herself onto her knees, and I found myself staring into those same eyes, but perhaps I had imagined the accusation I thought I'd seen before. Instead, now she seemed resigned. She laid a bundle at my feet and begged me to accept her son's gift."

Father waved a servant forward. The gift, if indeed that was what she carried, filled her arms, and she seemed relieved to set it down beside Maram.

"Is this it?" Maram asked, her hand hovering over the coarse cloth wrapping the item.

Father nodded.

Maram twitched back a corner of the cloth, then gasped in surprise. She peeled away the wrappings until she had revealed the whole thing, though she didn't dare touch it. To touch it would be to spoil its magnificence.

The jewelled thing looked like a blackberry bush from the cold climates far to the north, with ripe fruit begging to be picked and flowers promising more for tomorrow. And so lifelike – whoever had crafted this knew the real thing. Why, she could almost taste the delicious sweetness on her tongue, a delight she had not known for far too long. She reached out to touch a berry, the reassuringly cold jewel reminding her that this cunning creation was not real.

"Who made this?"

"I do not know, for she did not say. All she said was that it was a gift from her son."

Maram's eyes met her father's. "Who is her son, who can afford to part with such a priceless gift? And why does his mother wear cheap widow's weeds when he has the coin for such magnificence?"

"I will find out on the morrow, for I have invited the man to a private audience with me."

Maram blew out her breath in a rush. Disappointment clouded her face. "Is that all you have to tell me?"

Father laughed. "Indeed it is. Like the audiences of the legendary storytellers of old, you must wait another day to find out what happens next." He rose to depart.

"Wait, Father, you forgot your shrub." She cradled the treasure in her arms, and offered it up to him.

He smiled. "You keep it. I see in your eyes you appreciate its beauty truly, like your mother would have. Consider it a wedding gift, for something tells me it should be."

He left, but Maram scarcely noticed, so busy was she in examining her new work of art. For that's what it was. A precious thing – why would anyone part with it, unless they needed to sell it to live?

What kind of man gave such a gift?

She wished she'd thought to ask her father to be present at tomorrow's audience, so that she might see the man for herself. But Father would have asked her to be there if he'd wanted her presence. He valued her opinion, and if he meant to keep this man at his court, she would meet him soon enough.

And when she did, Maram resolved to ask him who his jeweller was, so that she might give the jeweller's name to Hasan and insist he create a garden of such things in her palace. One such shrub would bankrupt him for sure.

Best not to have Hasan assassinated yet, then. First he had to build her a ruinously expensive palace. With emphasis on the ruin.

Twenty

"Master, your palace is complete," Aladdin heard the djinn say.

He wrenched his eyes open and wished he hadn't. The predawn light told him it was far too early an hour for anyone to be about. But he remembered Kaveh's warning, so he rose and dressed. "Show it to me, then," he said.

The djinn waved his arm and a portal opened up in the east wall through which he could see the darkness of some other place entirely, instead of the rising sun he knew would be hitting that wall. The djinn bowed. "After you, master."

Reluctantly, Aladdin stepped through the wall, from his mother's tiny house to a cool, spacious hall. Oh, this was exactly the sort of place where Maram belonged. Mosaic tiles stretched up the walls and across the ceiling, mirroring the night sky over the desert. Even the tiles underfoot were the exact colour of the desert sands.

The djinn said nothing as Aladdin crept from room to room, unable to keep himself from staring. Having never seen the Sultan's palace, he hoped this would be good enough. It was certainly better than anything he'd seen in the prince's apartments in Tasnim. The bathhouse was an exact replica of the one where he'd first met Maram, including the towel storage alcove where he'd hidden. The djinn had not forgotten towels, either – the soft cloths were piled high, waiting for their royal mistress.

Aladdin took a deep breath, and lost himself in memories of that day. He'd spent one perfect day with her, and it would have to be enough. She would live here with her new husband, and be so happy she never thought of Aladdin again.

"You must see your audience chamber, master," the djinn said.

Aladdin opened his mouth to say that no part of this palace was his, but there would be time for that later. Instead, he followed the djinn up a curving flight of stairs to the level above.

The djinn had timed his entrance perfectly. As Aladdin stepped out of the archway into the hall, the morning sun hit the windows in a blaze of magnificence. For unlike the other windows in the city, these were closed in panes of glass and translucent gemstones. A veritable rainbow of colours cascaded down the walls to the floor, before dancing up to the ceiling from cleverly placed mosaic tiles that reflected light everywhere. A room designed to dazzle, which indeed it did.

Aladdin lifted a hand to his eyes, lest he be blinded by so much brightness. "Now show me the garden."

"Allow me," Kaveh said, leading Aladdin down the stairs again and into a courtyard in the heart of the palace. At first glance, he'd created what appeared to be a real garden, but when the morning sun touched the trees, it shattered that illusion into a thousand beams of light. Each berry and flower seemed to take on its own glow, glittering in harmony with each leaf and trunk, but it was nowhere near as blinding as the audience hall above. This place held a welcoming glow, inviting him to linger a little longer. Oh, if only he could, but this place was not for the likes of him. It would house Maram and her new husband.

"It's perfect," Aladdin said, and was surprised to see both djinn swell with pride at the compliment. "I have another request. Is there any way I can see Maram's betrothed?" Seeing the man who had won the heart of the lovely princess would remind Aladdin why he would never be good enough for her, or this palace.

"I shall bring him here directly," the djinn

said, opening a hole in the wall.

"No! I don't want him to know I'm there. I want to see him in his home, where I imagine he'd be asleep now," Aladdin clarified.

Kaveh bowed. "I'd be honoured to help you. Invisibility is my speciality."

Leaving the other djinn behind with his handiwork, Kaveh and Aladdin made their way through the near-empty streets to the Vizier's house, where the princess's soon-to-be husband lived. They entered the house and dodged between servants readying the house for the day. No one spared them a glance, buoying Aladdin's hopes that Kaveh had made them truly invisible.

"The best bedchamber is this way," Kaveh said softly, leading Aladdin upstairs. "Don't worry, they can't hear us."

"How do you know where it is? Have you been here before?" Aladdin asked.

"This house has belonged to a long line of viziers. The man in office may change but the house does not."

One day, Aladdin would ask Kaveh how old

he was. Today was not that day, though, as he fought to catch his breath while they hurried up the stairs.

Aladdin heard quiet sobbing, then a smack of flesh on flesh followed by a pained cry, like a child being spanked. Curiosity made him follow the sound into a grand bedchamber, but the scene he found made him wish he hadn't.

A semi-naked slave girl, judging by what remained of her torn clothes, squirmed under a naked man who evidently took great pleasure in her tears and cries of pain as he bedded her. He clenched his fingers around her breast, squeezing until she let out a little scream, then backhanded her across the face, adding what would be another bruise to match her two blooming black eyes.

"You like that, don't you, slut of a sultan's daughter? Answer me!" the man demanded. He hit her again, twice, eliciting more cries of pain. "Answer me!"

Finally, the weeping girl whimpered, "Yes, master. Your touch honours me."

"Louder!" he insisted, slapping her face

again.

Her voice rose to a shriek as she repeated the words, over and over, at his command, each sentence punctuated by another blow from the brute.

Aladdin wanted to help the girl, but what could he do? He was half the man's size, and there were dozens of servants who would come to his assistance. Why weren't they coming to help the girl? For surely they could hear her…

He stuck his head out of the open doorway. Sure enough, a steady stream of servants filed past, intent on their tasks for the day.

The girl screamed, and Aladdin saw a serving girl flinch. She stumbled, then caught herself and continued past, hugging her arms to her chest. Arms bruised almost black in places, Aladdin noticed, matching her own fading black eyes.

All the female servants bore the marks of this monster, he realised. All were young and pretty, or would be if not for the bruises. No older women worked here.

"Is that the Vizier?" Aladdin asked. Even as the words left his lips, he knew they could not be true. The brute had not looked old enough to be the father of an adult son, old enough to marry Maram. Dread curled a cold tendril around his heart.

"No, that is his son, Hasan, who will soon marry the princess," Kaveh said sadly.

Aladdin swore. "Not while I live, he won't. If he lays so much as a finger on her perfect skin, I will kill him myself."

How did a humble spinner's son stop the daughter of the Sultan from marrying whoever she wished? The Sultan would not listen to him. Perhaps if he was the Vizier's equal, or a prince…

A bubble of inspiration burst in Aladdin's head, brighter than dawn in his own audience chamber. For it would be.

"Kaveh, go to the alley behind the entrance to the marketplace. There you will find a number of men waiting to be offered work. Labourers, all of them. Tell them you come from me, and you will pay them a week's wages if they meet me at the gates of the city an hour before my audience with the Sultan."

"What will you be doing?"

"Persuading the servant of the lamp to make me look like the richest prince in the world. One who deserves not only that palace, but the princess, too."

Kaveh grinned. "That's the spirit. I still haven't seen this princess of yours yet."

Twenty-One

"Leave me," Maram commanded her attendants, and they did, leaving her alone in the bathhouse.

Except…she wasn't really alone.

"You may approach," she said softly.

A dark-clad figure melted out of the shadows. "I was informed you might have a job for me."

Maram turned a seductive smile on the hooded man. She did not need to see his face as long as he could see hers. "There is no might about it. If you are indeed the best assassin in the city, then I have a job for you."

"There is no assassin better than me," the man said.

Maram knew it was a lie, but this man probably did not. The best assassin she knew was out of the city, with no definite return date, so second best must do.

"Then tell me. If someone paid you to assassinate the Sultan, how would you do it?" she asked.

The man shook his head. "I would not take that job."

"What about the Vizier?"

"He is an old man. Old men are prone to clumsiness. If old age does not carry him off, perhaps he might stumble down some stairs, or trip and hit his head."

The stories Maram had heard about this man were true. He was clever enough to make cold-blooded murder appear like an accident.

"And what about the Vizier's son?"

"He is young and strong, but death lurks in the most unlikely places. One of his servants might slip poison into his wine, for it is well known that he is a hard master."

"What if someone asked you to kill a princess?"

"You toy with me, Your Highness. I could kill you now where you stand, for you carry no weapon. By the time your servants came to your assistance, you would be dead." He bowed his head. "But an assassin with my skills has the freedom to choose which jobs he takes. And I would not wish to rob the world of your beauty, so you are safe from me. I do not kill women."

She had heard this, too.

"What poison would Hasan's servants choose, I wonder?" she said.

The assassin produced a small pouch. "A little will send him to sleep, but enough will make sure he does not wake up."

Maram nodded, satisfied. "Then I will pay you for it now, and on the night before my wedding, I ask you to meet me here once more, to complete the job." She held out a jingling purse.

He exchanged his pouch for the purse, then paused to count his coins. "This is more than my usual fee."

"You will receive the same again when your job is complete."

He bowed deeply. "As Your Highness commands." He melted into the shadows once more.

When she was certain he'd gone, Maram peeped into the pouch. She almost laughed. He'd given her opium, a drug she'd used more often than any other. A waste of good coin, but never mind. She had no doubt Hasan used the stuff, too, so it would be no surprise if anyone found the pouch in his house. Or in hers.

She left the bathhouse deep in thought, only to find her guards on the steps outside, holding back a crowd.

"What's going on?" Maram asked, craning her neck to see past her men.

"There's some sort of procession in the street. Everyone's lined up to see some prince come to visit your father."

She wasn't sure which of her men had spoken, for they were too intent on the street below to turn when they spoke to her. Gross disrespect she could have the man killed for, she knew, but Maram understood men better than most. Curiosity was a powerful thing, and she had no desire to inspire enmity in her father's guards. If she killed Hasan, she would need them to be sympathetic to her, or they might suspect.

"A gold coin to the first man to tell me the prince's name, and where he comes from!" she cried, pulling the coin from her purse.

A shout came from the crowd: "The Prince of Tasnim!"

More shouts followed the first, but none seemed to know more than the name of his principality. It was enough. She handed the coin to one of her guards, who saw it went to its rightful owner.

She need not have bothered. The prince's entourage appeared then, gaudily dressed men who threw fistfuls of coins into the crowd. Maram did not recognise the livery, for that was what it was – these richly dressed men were the prince's servants.

After them came dancers, whirling in unison, so that their veils and skirts spun like tops. Finally, there were ranks of what she thought were porters, if a lowly porter could afford the silks these men wore. On their heads, they carried dishes piled high with gems much like those she'd seen on the jewelled shrub her father had shown her.

Behind the porters rode a man on a horse so pale it appeared white – something no horse could in the desert, for the sands coloured everything they touched. But they could not touch this animal, as fine as any in her father's stable.

The man…no, the prince, for he wore a crown nestled in the folds of his turban, threw coins into the crowd, too, earning a rousing cheer from everyone as he passed. Maram tried to get a glimpse of his face, to see if he was one of the princes she knew, but the cheering, waving townspeople made that impossible.

The prince passed, followed by another

company of coin-throwing servants, and the crowd closed ranks behind him to join the parade to the palace.

Maram cursed inwardly and waited a long time until the road cleared before she commanded her men to clear a path for her to go home. Whoever this prince was, he'd intended to make a spectacle of himself, and she would soon know far more about him than she cared to.

Twenty-Two

When Aladdin prostrated himself before the Sultan, he had a sudden image of the Sultan commanding one of the guards to lop off his head before he could rise.

No, he told himself. The Sultan was a wise and just ruler. He'd wait for Aladdin to speak and say something wrong before he executed him. Some reassurance. More than ever, Aladdin wanted to take to his heels and run home, but he knew he could not. He had to save Maram from that man.

"Rise," the Sultan commanded.

Aladdin rose onto his knees. "You Majesty, in thanks for your kind invitation, I have brought you a gift." He waved Berk and his men forward. They laid their baskets of jewels at the Sultan's feet, then bowed again.

The Sultan's eyes gleamed almost as brightly as the jewels he surveyed. "Such a generous gift demands another in return. What would you ask of me, Prince of Tasnim?"

Kaveh's whispers in the crowd had reached the Sultan's ears, then, as he'd promised.

"I ask for the Princess Maram's hand in marriage."

The Sultan's eyebrows rose. "But she is already betrothed to another."

No, she was betrothed to a beast of a man who did not deserve her. "So I have heard, but I understand there is a condition on the betrothal. Namely, her husband must build her a palace befitting such a priceless princess before the marriage can take place." He saw the Sultan open his mouth to respond, so Aladdin hastily added, "I propose a contest between her betrothed and myself. Whoever can build a palace that meets with her approval first, will win her hand."

If the Vizier or his son were present, they would surely object, but the Sultan had granted Aladdin an audience alone, if the crowd he'd brought in his procession could be considered alone.

The Sultan eyed him. "My daughters are precious to me, especially Princess Maram. I would not bestow them lightly on a man I do not know. I will consider your proposal for a day, and give you my answer on the morrow." He gave a wave of dismissal to signal the end of the brief audience.

"Thank you, Your Majesty. But if I may add one thing…I took the liberty of building a palace beside your own which I had hoped would satisfy the princess. If you are of a mind to accept my proposal, I humbly request that Her Highness tell me how poorly I may have anticipated her wishes on the morrow." Aladdin held his breath. He had little hope that Maram would be present tomorrow, but if the

Sultan denied that part of his request, he might be more inclined to accept the rest.

"We shall see."

Indeed we shall, Aladdin thought, as he and his men backed out of the audience chamber. Tomorrow could not come too soon.

Twenty-Three

Maram stabbed the needle through her embroidery, wishing she'd chosen to attend court today instead of going to the bathhouse to meet with the assassin. Now she'd have to wait until her father retired for the day before she heard what the prince had said.

"Are you thinking of becoming an assassin? I've heard tales of men in the far east who execute traitors by piercing them with a thousand needles."

Maram dropped the needle in surprise.

"Father?"

"I have another gift for you today, but it will not fit in here. You must come with me if you wish to see it."

A squad of guards waited outside, and Maram hastily secured her veil, realising they would be leaving the palace, for neither she nor her father required an escort so large within the palace grounds.

Father filled her in as they walked. The prince had asked for her hand, and promised her a palace, just as she'd asked for from Hasan.

"A palace he tells me he has already built – here," Father said with a flourish as the building came into view.

Maram's breath caught in her throat. How had she missed it this morning? Too intent on her thoughts, she supposed, as her men fought their way through the crush outside the palace.

A second palace sat beside her father's, grand and gleaming in the sun. The open gates beckoned her in, and Maram could not refuse the elegant invitation. The scent of rosewater reached her nostrils — whoever owned the palace had seen fit to perfume the entrance steps, a delightful touch.

As she stepped inside, she expected servants to come rushing forward to greet her and offer refreshments, yet there was no sound but the echo of her and her father's footsteps on the tiles. They were alone in this palace. A palace that easily outshone her father's.

The tiled floors were so perfectly smooth, they seemed to be made of a single piece of stone. Every room had a different ceiling mosaic, so lifelike it seemed she was staring up at the real sky and not a picture of it. And the bathhouse…tears sprang to her eyes to see her dreams made real, in a way no man could have known she wanted, for she hadn't even told her father how much she wanted this. The bathhouse was as opulent as the rest of the palace, but it was also familiar — if the bathhouse she'd visited that very morning were made anew, then surely it would look like this. A copy of the place on the day it opened, all those centuries ago…but no one could know such things!

Shaking her head at the impossibility of what her eyes were telling her, Maram no longer knew what to think.

"Come and look at the garden," her father called.

Only now did Maram realise she stood alone in the bathhouse – her father had ventured into the courtyard without her.

A courtyard or a garden? Maram wasn't certain until she saw the light glint off what she'd taken for grass. No, the ground was covered in grass-coloured tiles, while jewelled shrubs and trees dotted the courtyard like the harem gardens at home. A jewelled replica of the harem gardens…a place no prince had ever visited, for her brothers had been given their own garden for their boisterous play. The only men who had ever visited them were sultans, like her father, or traitors like her mother's lover, Amani. There was magic at work here. Magic meant to delight her, and her alone.

Maram's mouth was unbearably dry. More than ever, she wished for a servant to offer her refreshment, but no one granted her wish.

"Father, whoever this man is…whoever built this…I must meet him," she said. Because if he was even the slightest bit better than Hasan, she would scream her YES to his proposals before he could repeat them to her.

A shape stepped out of the shadows. A shape wearing a crown in the folds of his turban. The prince threw himself face down on the green tiles. "I am honoured by the presence of such a beautiful princess and her father in my humble home."

Maram glanced around, only to find her father nowhere in sight. Had he gone, leaving her alone with this man?

It seemed he had.

Maram took a deep breath. "Rise, Prince of Tasnim, for I am the one who is honoured. Why would a man I barely know offer me such a magnificent gift?"

"Because Hasan does not deserve you." The prince rose stiffly to his feet, only to lose his turban partway up. It clanged to the tiles, crown first, and rolled away.

She couldn't hide her smile. "And you do?"

"No," he said, raising his head to meet her eyes. "But I could think of no other way to free you of both slavery and your betrothal to him."

Maram's breath caught in her throat and she couldn't seem to draw another one. This couldn't be. It couldn't. Yet...

"Aladdin?" she gasped.

<h1 style="text-align:center">Twenty-Four</h1>

Aladdin stood invisible by Kaveh's side, watching the Sultan and Princess Maram marvel over the palace the two djinn had built. Now, Aladdin truly believed she was as precious to her father as he'd said. The Sultan spent more time watching his daughter's reactions than looking at the place. She meant more to him than whatever diplomatic assistance she provided to the court.

For a moment, he wished he'd told the Sultan about Hasan instead of creating such an elaborate scheme. He would never give the daughter he loved to that man if he truly knew what Hasan would do to her.

"What? Did you spot a mistake in the tiles?" Kaveh demanded. "Why do you look so miserable?"

"I should have asked the Sultan to call off the engagement, not offered a new one. She will see through this for sure." He waved at his silk clothes. They felt so slippery against his skin he worried they would slip right off and leave him naked. Not that it mattered when he was unseen, but…

"Don't be daft," Kaveh snapped. "Once the Sultan's given his word to the Vizier, he can't break the engagement, unless a better offer comes along. You made him the only offer he could accept. And once he sees the audience chamber, he will."

"But the princess will hate me for trying to deceive her. I'd hate me for making a bargain with her father without knowing I had her consent first. If there was a way I could speak to her before her father…"

Kaveh nodded. "Here she comes. I'll take him up to see the audience chamber, and you take a moment with your princess." He strode across the courtyard and materialised on the steps to the upper levels. He bowed deeply. "Your Majesty, my master bade me to greet you and show you anything you wish to see. I would recommend the audience chamber…"

The Sultan cut him off. "I had begun to think the palace was empty. Let us see this chamber." He headed up with Kaveh.

"Father, whoever this man is…whoever built this…I must meet him," Maram said, stepping into the sun. She blinked, blinded.

Aladdin could not have asked for a better opportunity than this. He threw himself at Maram's feet.

At her command, he rose, taking his time to meet her eyes and the complete lack of recognition he expected to see there. A princess would not remember a poor boy she'd met in the bathhouse.

"Aladdin?" His name was music on her lips.

He wanted to sink to his knees again, and

give thanks to whatever deity had helped him this time. But he forced himself to stay on his feet, for she had ordered it.

"How did you manage to build such a place? So lavish, so perfect, so fast?" she asked. "When I last saw you, you hadn't eaten for days, yet now..." She ran a hand down his tunic.

So that's why royalty wore silk. The feel of her fingers through it was pure bliss. Aladdin wanted to moan in pleasure, but he knew he only had a moment before her father returned. "I cannot tell you, for you would not believe me. I scarcely believe it myself. What I can tell you is that I ventured out into the desert and found a priceless treasure. A treasure that made all this possible, though it nearly killed me to return here. It's for you, Princess. All of it. If there is anything you wish changed, name it, and it shall be done. You don't even need to accept me – the palace is my gift to you. All I ask in return is that you don't marry that brute, Hasan."

Maram's eyes hardened. "Why would I not

want the man who risked his life for me, to give me this, to save me from that brutish fool? I've been to the bathhouse every day, sent men out looking for you…by all that's holy…" She tore the veil from her head and threw it on the tiles. Maram shook her hair off her face – a night-dark river Aladdin longed to stroke – then wrapped her arms around Aladdin and kissed him.

She tasted sweeter than before, more intoxicating than the finest wines in Tasnim, and more arousing than any of the erotic murals in the prince's harem. The softness of her body in his arms made him wonder if he truly had died and gone to paradise after all.

"Maram!"

At the Sultan's exclamation, Aladdin reluctantly released his angel and held his arms out wide in surrender.

Maram waited to finish one last kiss before she unwound her arms from Aladdin. "What, Father? I'm going to marry this man. He'll see more than my face and hair, soon enough." She bent to retrieve her veil, trailing her fingers across Aladdin's groin. "Soon enough," she repeated softly.

Aladdin's cheeks grew as heated as…he could hardly face the Sultan while he had a tent in his accursed silk pants. A normal tunic would have hidden everything, but in this finery…he forced himself to retrieve his turban and hold it before his groin to hide the effect Princess Maram had on him.

She winked as she wound her veil around her hair, leaving her face uncovered. "Prince Aladdin wishes to know if any improvements should be made to his palace. It appears perfect to me, but you have seen more of it than I have."

The Sultan stared from Aladdin to Maram. "What about Hasan?"

She frowned. "What about him, Father? I doubt he has laid so much as a single stone on the palace he promised to build, but if I'm wrong, I will happily compare the two. We already know who will be the victor in any competition."

"What will I tell his father?"

Maram shrugged. "Tell him you received a better offer from a prince. He's your adviser. If he advised you to accept a vizier's son over a prince, he'd be a fool, and out of a job. You needn't tell him right away. I will need at least four weeks before my wedding. You'll have some time."

"Four weeks?" Aladdin blurted out.

Maram smiled mischievously. "Four weeks until the wedding, yes. It will take that long for my dress. A royal wedding is worth celebrating." She winked. "Don't worry, my prince. I shall have my things moved to your palace tonight. From this moment, I am yours."

Oh, how he longed for that to be true. But it was not. "No, you and this palace will not be mine until we are married. Until then, this palace belongs to you alone, Princess. I will stay with my mother but, with your permission, I shall visit you, if you wish."

Maram's shock brightened into a smile. "Oh, I do wish."

The Sultan coughed. "It seems my daughter

has made her decision, and what father would argue with a woman in love? Shall we meet on the morrow, Prince Aladdin, or will you accept my answer now?"

Aladdin bowed. "I will accept whatever Your Majesty is gracious enough to grant me."

The Sultan laughed. "My favourite daughter, it would seem. Just like her mother, I can refuse her nothing. But I will add one thing." His expression darkened. "If you hurt her, if my daughter sheds a single tear because of you, I will have your head severed from your body so fast, you will not have time to blink in surprise before your heart stops beating."

Aladdin met the Sultan's eye now, not a subject to his sovereign, but a future son-in-law to a protective father. "If I ever cause harm to come to Princess Maram, I will offer my head to you myself, for I will deserve such a fate."

He opened his mouth to ask what the Sultan would do to Hasan, but he'd taken his daughter's arm and already started walking away.

Hasan no longer mattered. Maram would marry him, and make Aladdin the happiest of men.

"I'd have risked killing myself, crossing the desert for her, too," Kaveh said fervently. "You are one lucky man."

Yes. Yes, he was.

Twenty-Five

When they returned to the Sultan's palace, Maram knew she would have a lot of questions to answer. But for the first time in longer than she could remember, she did not care. She'd seen him, she'd kissed him and by some incredible change of heart from fate, she'd get to keep him. Aladdin. The only man who'd ever touched her heart.

The only man who kissed her like he cared how he touched her, not wanting to consume her in his own blazing passion. Oh, Aladdin had passion enough, she was certain of it, for she'd seen it in his eyes as he kissed her.

But he didn't want to marry her for himself. Oh, no. He wanted to save her from Hasan. One day she would tell him how she'd planned to save herself, but not until after they were married. She didn't want to frighten him. Then again, Aladdin was not some soft courtier, to be frightened by a woman who took her fate into her own hands. No, he was a man who would risk everything – even his own life – for the woman he loved.

Her mouth became dry. Did he love her? He had not said so, but then he'd hardly had the chance to do so. Yet why else would he risk so much for her, if not for love?

"How do you know this man, and why have I never heard of him?" Father demanded.

Maram blinked. She'd been so lost in thought she hadn't realised they'd arrived in her private apartments, and they were alone. She pulled off her veil and shook out her hair. She would have to be careful, for her father thought Aladdin was a prince, and she had no desire to tell him otherwise.

"I met him once, briefly. I liked him very much then and I believe he liked me, too, but as neither of us were in a position to marry at the time, I thought such a thing would never happen. Evidently I underestimated both his affection and his wealth." She blew out a breath. She would not make that mistake again. Aladdin was not a man to be underestimated at all.

"What about Hasan? Why would you agree to marry Hasan if you loved this man so much?" Father persisted.

Ah, here was the crux of the matter. She was her mother's daughter, after all.

"I never intended to marry Hasan. He is a vicious brute who beats his servants and has wanted to do the same to me since the moment we met. I had hoped to bankrupt him by forcing him to build a palace that I would never be satisfied with. Then, when he was so deeply in debt he could no longer continue, perhaps he would give up his suit, and he'd be forced to release the servants he has abused for so long."

Father's eyebrows rose so high they disappeared into his jewelled turban. "How did I not know this about him?"

Maram lifted her shoulders in a delicate shrug. "Perhaps only women gossip about such things, or perhaps he hides it well from anyone outside his household. But you sent him with me on a trading expedition, where he tried to turn me into his whore. He did not succeed, and has hated me ever since. I had no idea you were unaware of his true nature, Father." Though it didn't surprise her. Vizier Ali must have known, and worked hard to conceal it from the Sultan.

He frowned, evidently deep in thought.

Maram let the silence build. Her father would fill it when he chose to.

Finally, he said, "So you don't wish to marry Hasan, but you do want this other man? This prince? He will make you happy?"

"Yes, Father. Aladdin will make me happy." He already had.

"But he will take you away from me, to his

own kingdom."

Maram had never seen her father pout before, but he looked dangerously close to doing so now. "Father, I will make it my mission to make sure Aladdin likes it so much here in our city, that he never wants to leave his palace. You will have to travel a little further to see me, but not so far as you think."

He nodded. "I'll summon Hasan and his father, and tell them the news. They certainly won't be happy when they hear."

No, they would not. Especially Hasan.

"Can you wait until I have left the palace, Father? I fear Hasan's anger will make him do something…reckless, when he hears the news."

The Sultan smiled fondly. "Of course. I will wait two days – will you be ready then?"

Maram nodded. She was so used to travelling, she and her servants could have her room stripped in an hour, if need be, to catch the tide. But never before had she felt that leaving a room would change her life forever. Now, there would be no returning from a future that was so unknown. Could anyone truly be ready for anything the future held?

"I shall," she vowed.

Twenty-Six

All the way home, Aladdin should have been walking on air, but he couldn't help but worry. The man he'd seen this morning, beating his slave, would not like losing Maram. What man would?

If another man – a real prince, perhaps – were to appear in the palace and persuade the Sultan that HE was a better match than either Aladdin or Hasan, Aladdin would not simply stand by and accept it. Not unless he truly believed someone could make Maram happier than he could.

The moment he got home, he dug out the lamp and summoned the djinn. Without waiting for the djinn to ask for orders, Aladdin said, "I need you to protect the princess in the palace you built. She'll bring her own staff, I'm sure, but she'll need guards and…I don't know what. And you. If all else fails, I need you to protect her."

"As you command, master. If I may suggest…"

Aladdin looked up. The djinn wasn't normally any more helpful than he needed to be. Not like Kaveh. "Yes?"

The djinn ducked his head. "I suggest placing the lamp in the palace treasury, so I will always be close by if Princess Maram needs me."

Something in the djinn's tone made Aladdin suspicious. "You are not to speak to her, interact with her in any way, or permit her to see you, unless her life depends upon it," Aladdin added.

This didn't seem to upset the djinn at all.

"Yes, master."

Aladdin decided he must have imagined it.

"If I may not speak to her…can you tell me if she liked the palace?"

Aladdin hesitated for a moment, but he couldn't see any reason not to answer. "Yes, she did. So much that she agreed to marry me because of it."

"Does she not reside in her father's palace?"

"Of course she does."

"Then why would she want another?"

Aladdin squinted at the djinn. He sure had a lot of questions about Maram. "Something about bankrupting the brute who expected to marry her. Not me, the other guy."

The djinn roared with laughter. "Oh, she is her mother's daughter. So ruled by passion, she would rather ruin a man than kill him outright. I would prefer a clean death, myself."

Feeling he was missing something that the djinn deliberately chose not to share, Aladdin told the djinn to hide in the lamp so that he might take him to his new home in the palace. The princess's palace. In four short weeks, it would be his, too. He'd need to find a more suitable place for his mother, as well. The tiny house they'd moved to after his father died had never felt like home, and he owed his mother more than this place. A palace of her own, perhaps, or an apartment in Maram's. He'd ask her when he saw her.

In the meantime, Aladdin made his way through the city. He'd persuaded Kaveh to find him some more suitable clothes than the embarrassing silk suit he'd worn for his triumphal entry into the city, and Kaveh had provided him with a fine linen tunic with matching turban and trousers. At first glance, they were no different to his normal clothes, but Aladdin could feel the difference. There were coins that jingled in his pockets, too, courtesy of the djinn who'd also filled the treasury in the palace with enough wealth to do him for several lifetimes.

And all because he'd accepted a job from that madman, Gwandoya. Who could still be trying to recruit men to do his dirty work, Aladdin realised. He had to warn Berk and the others.

He made his way to the alley where they would normally be, but the alley was empty. Of course, they'd done their day's work in the procession this morning. He hoped Kaveh had paid them well for it. None of them had recognised him in his finery, and he hadn't dared to climb down off his horse once he was on it so that he might speak to them. The beast had proved just as challenging to ride as a camel. Henceforth, Aladdin swore to walk on his own two feet, wherever he went.

And his feet would lead him back to the alley on the morrow, for Berk deserved to know he'd been right about Gwandoya.

When he arrived at the palace gates, he found a steady stream of servants carrying things from the Sultan's palace to Maram's, before returning for more.

He found her in a set of apartments overlooking the garden. "Why did you not choose the best bedchamber?" he asked as he entered. "Unless your father plans to move into your palace with you, you will be the highest ranking inhabitant of the house."

She laughed. "Not so. You're royalty, too, remember – I left the best apartment for you. Though I hope to be invited in there often. Every night, in fact."

Her kiss didn't take him by surprise, but it seemed to melt things inside him that had no business melting. "Princess, this palace is yours, and you are free to go wherever you wish."

"What about in here?" She slid a hand under his tunic, then frowned as she encountered something hard. "What is this?"

Not what she had hoped for, certainly. Aladdin pried the lamp from her fingers. "It is…a lucky talisman, that has protected my house and now will protect yours. I'll just put it in the entry hall…" He found a suitable alcove high on the wall, and tucked the lamp into the back of it. "There. Now you will be safe." Oh, how fervently he hoped that would be the case.

"Now, you can invite me to your chamber," Maram said.

More than anything, he wanted to do just that. To take this beautiful woman and anything she offered.

"Not yet. It would be dishonourable to do so before we are married," Aladdin said with considerable regret.

She laughed. "I am not some blushing virgin, as you well know. We are promised, and I know you are a man of your word. I promise our nights together will be the greatest pleasure you have ever known."

Aladdin swallowed. Every word was the truth, and yet…

"You may not be a virgin, but I am, and I fear my clumsiness will make you wish to break your promise. I am not worthy of you. Not yet."

Her eyes mesmerised him like never before. "What if I told you I knew a spell that could guarantee when you make love to the woman of your heart's desire, she will know nothing but pleasure at your touch?"

His mouth was too dry to speak. He tried twice before he had to clear his throat to get the words out. "Keep your spell for our wedding night, for you will need it then. Please, Princess."

She stared at him for a long time, then nodded. "All right. If you wish. I have never had to wait for a man before and I find I do not like it. However, I believe you will be worth the wait, so I shall."

If Aladdin looked at her for any longer, he would be lost in her eyes, and he would agree to anything she desired, for he desired it, too. He bade her a hasty farewell and hurried out before he could surrender to her.

It was a long walk home, but he noticed little of it, for his thoughts were filled with Maram, and their future nights together. The desert heat was cold in comparison.

Twenty-Seven

For two days, Aladdin did not visit her, and it drove Maram mad. She'd seen him again, and kissed him. She'd kissed him so many times he heated her blood near to boiling, and still he resisted her. Not even their betrothal was enough to bring him to her bed. If she didn't know better, she'd swear the man had seduction magic of his own, but she'd never met a man so frightened of intimacy before. Clumsy, indeed. She'd known clumsy, and he wasn't. His every kiss was perfect — making love to him would be even more perfect.

Yet still he did not come, and it was her turn to fear. Had she driven him away with her persistence? Or did he have other matters to attend to? For she knew he was no prince, not truly, so his money must come from somewhere. When she saw him next, she would ask about it, and this time, she would not rest until she had her answer.

Darkness crept over the city on the second day, dulling her spirits until Maram had scarcely any appetite for her evening meal.

A cacophony of banging and shouting sounded outside, and Maram sent a maid to find out what was going on.

Another maid came skidding into the room, wide-eyed. "Your Highness, he's here!"

So Aladdin surprised her servants, did he? "Send him in," Maram said, calling for a second place to be set at her table for her soon-to-be husband.

The first one returned, laughing. "There is a madman outside, rattling a great bundle of new lamps all tied together, offering to trade new lamps for old. There is an old lamp in the entrance hall. I found it while I was cleaning. Shall I take it to him and see if he will truly trade it, as he says?"

Maram no longer cared about whatever was going on outside. "Fine, fine," she said vaguely, combing her fingers through her hair. Did she have time to summon a servant with a comb to do a proper job? She had not expected Aladdin to come so late, and she did not want him to find her looking anything but her best.

"What is this I hear that you are to marry some prince? You are promised to me!"

Hasan burst into the room, his eyes as wild as any madman outside.

Maram cautiously rose to her feet, so that she might run if she needed to. "My father, the Sultan, controls my fate, as he rules over us all," she said slowly. There were no guards in her private chambers. Her only weapon was a small eating dagger, and even that lay on the table where she'd left it.

"You're mine! Mine!" Hasan spat, striding forward.

Maram scuttled back, hoping she had judged the entrance to the gardens right. Once she reached the darkness, she could turn and run, and perhaps hide.

Her back hit the wall. Oh, by all that was holy, she had the worst luck. Maram edged to her left, closer to Hasan, but also closer to freedom.

Not close enough. His meaty hands closed around her throat and choked off her air.

"You belong to me, not some foreign prince!"

Colour leached away from Maram's vision as she struggled to breathe. Hasan would kill her after all and she and Aladdin would never…she'd never…

"You dare to steal from me!" a new voice roared.

Hasan threw her to the floor, knocking the remaining breath from her lungs. Maram coughed and gasped and fought to stay conscious. She had to get to the knife…

"She is my bride, and no one else's!" Hasan shouted back, storming back the way he'd come.

Maram dragged herself across the floor and snatched the knife from the table. Thus armed, she subsided on the tiles, too exhausted to move any more just yet.

But she had to. Had to get up, be ready to run or defend herself, because if she didn't, Hasan would kill her for sure.

She drew in a great gulp of air, then another, and the second was somehow tainted with smoke. Fire. Faintly, she could hear her servants screaming, and the sound of running feet as they escaped the blaze now filling her palace with smoke.

She coughed, hard, tears blurring her vision. Maram grabbed the table and hauled herself into a sitting position, still coughing as the smoke grew too thick for her to see.

She must have hit her head, she decided, because she couldn't be seeing what she thought was before her. The smoke coalesced into a giant, blue man, who faced off against Hasan as though the two were about to fight.

"Kill the miserable thief. No one steals from

Gwandoya!" the unfamiliar male voice said.

Maram blinked, her vision clearing just in time to see the blue man clasp his hands together and bring them down on Hasan's head. Hasan's head burst like an overripe melon, bits of flesh splattering on the tiles, before his headless body collapsed amid the gore.

"Oh my God," Maram breathed, then clapped a hand over her mouth to muffle the scream that would not be silenced. The blue man had killed him, squashed him like an insect, all over her floor…

And she was next.

With a squeak, Maram leaped to her feet and bolted into the garden. She sank to her knees behind a shrub and hoped the shadows hid her from the blue man's sight.

Moments passed, and no one gave chase. She dared to breathe again.

"Servant of the lamp, I command you to take this palace and everyone in it, and carry it to my homeland," the unfamiliar man ordered.

"As you wish, master," boomed a voice that

could only belong to the blue giant.

Then the ground shook beneath Maram as though the palace had been hoisted on the back of a giant camel. She lost her balance, slamming her head against a tree, and darkness swallowed her whole.

Twenty-Eight

Getting measured up by another man while wearing little more than a loincloth was a new sensation to Aladdin, and he wasn't sure he particularly liked it, but Maram would expect him to wear nice clothes to their wedding, and probably afterwards, too, so he resigned himself to getting used to spending more time at the tailor shop. Besides, wishing for clothes from the djinn seemed even stranger, for Aladdin had no idea where the clothing came from. He hoped the djinn used magic to create it, but what if he stole it from someone? The Sultan or some other rich man might not notice a few missing tunics, but if he'd taken things from a merchant or tailor, that made Aladdin himself little better than a common thief. The two djinn had given him riches enough that he could afford to buy such things, so he should do so.

Not to mention he was certain the tradesmen and merchants who had been his father's friends before he died had provided charity to himself and his mother – a kindness he needed to repay. So if he'd ordered more tunics than he normally wore in a year…so what? He had the coin, and they wanted the business. He hadn't ordered anything but his wedding clothes made in silk, though, remembering the indecent way it had clung to him, especially when his desire for Maram had made him lose control. It would not happen again on their wedding day, he swore – he would be the picture of modest decorum.

Though he was finding it increasingly hard to stay away from her, in every sense of the word. He might not have shared her bed yet, but she certainly shared his – dominating his dreams every night. Aladdin knew he would pay her a visit today, and this time, he wasn't sure he could refuse her invitation to stay the night. Maram was intoxicating, in all the best ways.

Perhaps he would bring her a gift. He stopped in the bazaar to examine the caged birds, wondering which one she'd like. The jewelled garden would be better with some life in it. He wanted to get her a bird that would sing beautifully, but the only sound any of them seemed to want to make was a distressed peeping right now.

A streak of gold shot between the cages and pounced on a loose thread that hung from the hem of his tunic. A cat – the tiniest he'd ever seen. Aladdin caught the kitten and held it up to better inspect it. The little creature batted at his turban until a fold came loose, then sank its needle-like teeth into the corner.

"How much for this ferocious beast?" Aladdin asked the merchant who owned the menagerie.

"If you can keep the little menace from killing my exotic birds, you may have it as a gift," the man said. "I keep the mother for the mice, but she has so many babies, I fear the city will soon be overrun."

Aladdin tossed him a coin anyway, then tucked the kitten inside his tunic, where it promptly curled up and went to sleep.

Now he had to go to see Maram – before her present woke up and clawed through his clothes. Unable to wipe the grin from his face, Aladdin set off for the palace.

"Stop! Are you Prince Aladdin?" a voice demanded.

It was on the tip of his tongue to tell the truth and deny it, but Aladdin knew he had little to fear from the Sultan's guards now. Why, he would soon marry the man's daughter.

"I am he," he said grandly.

Two guards took his arms. "Then you must come with us. The Sultan commands it." They marched him the shortest way to the Sultan's palace, away from Maram.

Aladdin sighed. She would understand, surely.

The guards released him without warning, dropping him on the tiles of the Sultan's audience chamber. Instead of getting up, Aladdin merely bowed deeply. "How may I serve Your Majesty?"

"You can tell me where my daughter and her palace are!"

Aladdin wanted to laugh, but he restrained himself. "Her palace is beside your own, and no doubt Her Highness Princess Maram is inside it."

The Sultan made an exasperated sound. "Show him!"

Aladdin's guards hauled him to his feet and half carried him out of the hall to the gates of his palace. Or where the gates of his palace should be. Where the palace had stood only yesterday, now there was only bare earth, compressed under the weight of the absent palace.

One of the djinn had turned it invisible,

Aladdin decided, reaching for the gate he knew had to be there. But his fingers closed around nothing but air.

He didn't resist as the guards dragged him back to the Sultan and left him on the floor.

"Her servants tell hysterical tales of giants and magicians and blazes that smoke and do not burn. Complete nonsense, for something has driven them all mad and made them run from my daughter's service. But they all agree on one thing: she was in the palace when they left, and now there is no sign of the princess or her palace. Tell me where they are!" the Sultan demanded.

Aladdin raised his head. "I do not know."

"Tell me, or I shall instruct my guards to cut off your head. Last night, I bade good night to my daughter in that very palace you caused to be built overnight. Today, the palace is gone. My daughter is gone. And so is the Vizier's son, Hasan. No one else can tell my how a palace can appear in a night – and disappear just as quickly. Can you?"

"Magic," Aladdin croaked. He swallowed,

attempting to moisten his suddenly dry throat, then said it again. "No one could do such a thing without magic."

Was Hasan some sort of magician, who'd somehow stolen both the palace and Maram? If he had, Aladdin had to find her. The palace didn't matter, but Maram…she could not be left to the mercies of the man who had none.

"Are you a magician?" the Sultan thundered.

"No," Aladdin admitted.

"Do you know what the punishment is for stealing from your sovereign?"

Aladdin did not, but he was sure he wouldn't like it. "Your Majesty, I have stolen nothing from you. In fact, I am as incensed as you. Someone has stolen my palace and the woman I love. I ask for your leave to hunt down this thief, so that I may bring him to justice. Give me a month, and if I cannot find him, you may do as you wish with me."

"Why should I trust you? If I release you now, what assurance do I have that you will return in a month, or at all?"

Aladdin met the Sultan's eyes steadily.

"Because, Your Majesty, if I do not find her in that time, then I fear Princess Maram will be dead, and I will beg you to die so that I might join her."

The Sultan was silent for a long moment before he finally said, "Very well. But if you fail to return my daughter to me, you will not need to beg. Your death will be painful, I promise you."

"Thank you, Your Majesty." The words came out of his mouth, but Aladdin's thoughts were not in the Sultan's palace at all. Instead, they were with Maram, wherever she might be. He prayed Hasan had not hurt her yet, and that Aladdin would be in time to save her from him.

He had to be.

Twenty-Nine

Maram woke in her own bed, her head throbbing as though she'd attended one of those all-night feasts the northern kingdoms loved so much. The ones where wine flowed like water.

But if she had attended such a feast, there would be a naked man in her bed, and she would be wearing a lot less than she was now. Instead, she was alone, wearing the same clothes she'd worn yesterday. All she was missing was her shoes.

She rose and called for her servants, but received no answer. In fact, the palace was strangely quiet, as though she was alone, yet she could see daylight filtering through the windows. Her staff were never lazy – they would not be abed at this hour. One of her maids should have woken her hours ago.

Something was terribly wrong.

Maram crept out into the garden, which sparkled in the sun as though nothing had changed. She knew otherwise, though, touching her head where it hurt most. She'd hit her head on a tree. This morning, the trunk was marked with a streak of blood that had blackened in the sun. Maram had not imagined the events of last night.

That meant Hasan was…Hasan was…

She swallowed and squared her shoulders. She had to see it again to be sure.

Her feet made almost no sound as she traversed the cool tiles to the entrance hall. Her eyes scanned the floor for the spot where Hasan had fallen.

Where he'd splattered.

Her stomach roiled, but Maram refused to let the nausea rule her. His body had been right there…yet now the tiles were clean of blood and brains and whatever else was supposed to stay inside a man's head when he was alive.

She had not imagined it, Maram told herself. Perhaps that's where the servants were – called to her father's court to bear witness to the body they'd found. She should join them, for she'd seen the blue man kill Hasan with her own eyes.

Not that her father would believe there was such a thing as a giant blue man made of smoke. Maram herself didn't believe it, but if there had been some magic at work, then perhaps such a thing could exist. Such magic was beyond her, though.

She returned to her apartments and dressed carefully, for she had no servants to help her. No matter. She managed, as she always did.

With one final pat to make sure her veil was in place, Maram marched to the gate. She crossed the entrance hall without faltering, maintaining a steady trot as she descended the sunlit stairs into air that seemed distinctly cooler than usual.

Only when she reached the bottom of the stairs did she dare to look up into the street outside the palace gates.

But the street was gone. In its place, endless grassland stretched to the horizon, the straight line broken by a few scrubby trees. This was not the city or the desert she knew – it was somewhere else entirely, a country Maram, even in her extensive travels, had never visited before.

She heard a squeak, which drew her gaze back from the horizon to the gates. Someone's dogs were nosing something in the grass, so she took a step closer to investigate.

One of the dogs heard her, for it lifted its bloodied muzzle and mewed at her. It was the strangest dog she'd ever seen. Why, it sounded almost like…

A loud roar drowned out whatever thought she'd intended to have as a larger creature rose from the grass. This Maram could identify.

The lioness was leaner than the ones she'd seen in menageries across the world, but there was no mistaking the deadly intent in her eyes as she stalked. She appeared to be hunting, and the dogs were not dogs at all, but lion cubs, eating the remains of…Hasan.

If she'd had anything in her belly, Maram would have brought it up then and there.

She had no right to feel faint at the thought of someone killing the man, not when she'd been ready to hire an assassin to do the job for her, Maram told herself, but it was no use. Even she would have seen that the man was given a proper burial, not fed to someone's pet lions.

Except…there was something wild about this lioness that made her take another look. No chains or collars bound them. No fence or walls caged them. The lioness and her cubs were free as the air, which meant there was nothing stopping them from…from…

Maram scrambled up the steps, not daring to take her eyes off the lioness. She backed inside the palace, fingers scrabbling at the door so that she might shut it firmly behind her. Were there bars? Something to keep the lioness out?

"You should not leave the palace, Princess. It is not safe."

Maram whirled, pressing her back to the door. "Who is there?"

A figure stepped out of the shadows, then bowed. "I did not mean to frighten you."

The light coming through the windows hit him, and stole Maram's breath in the same moment.

"Are you going to kill me, too, like you killed Hasan?" she demanded of the blue man.

"He commanded me to protect you," the man said. As she watched, he shrank, until he was almost the size of an ordinary man. "Hasan deserved his fate."

She didn't argue. She, more than anyone, knew what Hasan was capable of. Perhaps the blue man was right.

The blue man swallowed. "You look just like her. Only more beautiful. How is that even possible?"

Maram knew only one woman who looked like her. "How do you know my mother?" she demanded, looking him in the eye for the first time. Only then did she falter, for recognition came as a shock. "Wait, Amani?"

He bowed his head. "I am."

"What are you doing here?"

"I am the slave of the lamp, which your betrothed kindly brought back to the city."

"Aladdin?"

Amani smiled faintly. "So that is his name. We were never properly introduced, and the enslavement spell on me is so strong I'm not sure I could call him anything but my master, anyway. He is a good man, a rare thing in these times, though I hope you will not be disappointed to discover that he is not a prince."

Maram wet her lips. "I already know. I met him before he left the city and found…wait, did you say a lamp?" She lifted her gaze to the alcove where Aladdin had placed his lucky lamp, but now the alcove was empty. "Where is it? He will be terribly disappointed that it is gone."

"Gwandoya the magician carries it with him, close to his heart. He is my master now, not Aladdin, though I wish it were otherwise. Gwandoya's desires run darker than Aladdin's simple tastes, and I fear what dark purpose he will use me for."

"Use you?" Maram ran through what Amani had told her, as well as her father, about his punishment for being the queen's lover. "Wait, you are a djinn, the servant of the lamp. No, the slave of the lamp, and your master is…the man who ordered you to kill Hasan."

Amani nodded. "I let him believe Hasan was your husband. I'm not sure he can tell the difference between him and Aladdin. The man is clearly mad."

"Where are we?"

"I am not sure what country this is, but we are many miles south from your home, far from any city."

Maram slumped. "So there is nowhere to escape to, even if the gates were not guarded by lions."

"The only way you will ever go home is if you persuade Gwandoya to order me to transport you or the palace back to your city." Amani smiled sadly. "If you have any of your mother's wiles to match her beauty, then I am sure you know how to make a man do whatever you wish."

Amani had known her as a child, so he had no idea how many men she'd seduced, all for her father's benefit and the good of the kingdom. What was one more, if it meant going home to Aladdin?

It would be a betrayal of Aladdin, and the freedom he had won for her. She had promised herself to him, and to let any other man touch her...Maram shivered. No, she could not even feign pleasure in any man's touch but his. Aladdin was the only man she wanted now, and she would not betray him with another, even if it meant their wedding would be delayed. She would return to him, somehow. There had to be a way. A way that did not involve seducing a madman.

Thirty

"Have you seen the palace that was here yesterday?" Aladdin asked. "It was here, but now it's gone." When the man shook his head, Aladdin tried another passerby. "Did you see anything here last night?"

People shook their heads and moved away from him, eyeing him suspiciously as they passed on the other side of the road.

Aladdin couldn't really blame them. After all, if he'd been confronted by a desperate man asking if he'd seen his palace, Aladdin might have thought him a madman, too. And it wasn't the palace he cared about as much as Maram. If Hasan had hurt her…he didn't know what he'd do.

He kept his head down as he ambled through the bazaar, not wanting to look at all the things he'd thought about buying for Maram.

"Aladdin? Is it really you?"

It took a moment for the sound of his name being called to penetrate through Aladdin's wretchedness, and it took another long moment before he raised his head to focus on the man calling. "Berk?"

Berk grinned. "We all thought the madman had killed you, like Bugra! Ah, you should have waited, for there was work enough for all of us earlier this week. Some foreign prince came to court one of the Sultan's daughters, and he needed porters to carry his treasures through the city before he made them a gift to the Sultan. Never have you seen such riches! Gold and jewels and all manner of precious things. He paid handsomely, too. So handsomely we hope he leaves soon, and needs our help again. That much coin would feed my family for a year."

"Did you see what happened to his palace?" Aladdin asked, hardly daring to hope.

Berk scratched his head, then righted his turban. "Not me. But one of Rasul's boys might have – they watch the place all day, ready to fetch the prince a porter if he needs one."

"All day? What about all night?"

Berk shrugged. "The boys go home for dinner after dark. Now their father can afford it."

Aladdin's heart sank. The boys wouldn't have seen anything if they weren't there.

"Hey, Rasul! Did your boys see anything strange about the prince's palace yesterday?" Berk shouted.

Rasul shrugged. "Ghulam said he saw a big nobleman go in to visit the prince. He challenged him, he said, shouting terrible things. Ghulam came running home, telling us we must help the prince fight the man off, or we would not see the prince again. As if the prince did not have his own guards to deal with such things."

Hasan. It had to be him.

"Did your boy see what happened to the palace?" Aladdin asked eagerly.

Rasul shook his head. "His mother had already made the evening meal. He stayed home to eat, like a good boy." He reflected for a moment, then added, "I hope the prince had guards. He pays better than the noblemen of this city. I would be disappointed if we don't see him again."

Berk clapped Aladdin on the shoulder. "Aladdin's the one we didn't think we'd see again. When he went off with that Gwandoya, we thought he'd be as doomed as the rest of them. Especially after Gwandoya came back without him, trying to get more of us to work for him. Yet here he is, safe and well. What sort of work did that madman want you to do, Aladdin? Was it as dangerous as we thought?"

Aladdin managed a smile. "Treasure hunting in the desert. So dangerous, when I got trapped, he left me for dead. I barely made it back. Whatever you do, don't agree to work for him. I was lucky to make it out alive from that place."

Berk nodded gravely. "I told you not to. None of us is that crazy. Although…I haven't seen him for the last couple of days. Have any of you?" The other men shook their heads. "Huh. Maybe he has a new employee to go treasure hunting for him. Hey, did you find anything?"

If he told the truth, every man here would head out into the desert to their deaths. Aladdin forced out a laugh. "Nothing but an old, tarnished lamp."

"Pity. We could all do with a change in fortune." Berk sighed. "Ah, well. When the prince leaves, make sure you're around. We'll tell him to hire you, too."

Aladdin thanked Berk, farewelled his friends, and headed home.

His mother was waiting for him. "What happened?" she demanded. "I heard some guards arrested you and took you to the palace!

I told you, only evil could come of messing with princesses and djinn. Djinn would try to trick the Sultan himself out of his crown, just for the fun of it. Or make his palace invisible. Or..."

That's how Hasan had done it. He'd somehow learned of the djinn that lived in the lamp, and enslaved him to his will. If the servant of the lamp could make a palace appear in a night, then surely he could make it disappear just as easily. He'd probably tried to keep Maram for himself.

Aladdin found his mother staring at him, as though expecting a reply. "You are wiser than I will ever be, Maman," he said warmly. He dug into his purse for his few remaining coins. "How about buying us a meal fit for a sultan tonight? I saw some new, exotic fruits in the bazaar this morning."

She looked slightly mollified. Wrapping her veil around her hair and face, she bade him farewell and headed out.

Aladdin let out a breath he hadn't known he'd been holding. "Kaveh, I need your help," he said.

The dejected djinn appeared beside him. "Before you ask, no, I can't bring your palace back, and as long as the other djinn has her, I can't bring your princess back, either. He's far more powerful than me."

Aladdin digested his words for a long moment before he said, "But you know where Maram and the palace are?"

Kaveh nodded. "In Gwandoya's homeland, deep in the savannah."

"Is Maram all right?" If she was, then nothing else mattered.

"I do not know."

"Take me to her," Aladdin said.

Kaveh threw his hands up in the air. "I told you, I am not as powerful as he is! Before he became a djinn, he was a powerful enchanter. One who knew portal magic and all manner of spells I have only heard of. I open doors and make things invisible. Even if I could get you there, what then? I am no match for the servant of the lamp. He will defeat me, and you, and then what will become of your princess?"

"Better to die than to stay here and do nothing. If we cannot reach her by magical means, there must be another way. I have a month to find her and bring her home, or I will die at the hands of the Sultan's executioner. Better to die trying to save her. And if I do, I ask only one more thing of you: deliver my head to the Sultan, with my humblest apologies for my failure."

Kaveh stared at him. "If that is your wish, master."

"It is."

Thirty-One

"Once again, I must remind you, Princess. Your husband is dead, and I am the only man you will ever see again. Will you finally accept me as your new husband?" Gwandoya asked.

Maram shook her head. "I cannot marry as long as I am in mourning. It is not seemly for me to take a new husband so soon."

"Who is there to know, or care? We are alone here!" Gwandoya snapped.

"As long as my late husband's shade haunts me, unable to find peace in the place where he was murdered, I cannot think to replace him."

Gwandoya jumped to his feet. "A pox on your husband's shade. Would that he were still alive, so that I might kill him more slowly, for he is such a thorn in my side that he deserves pain in equal measure!" He gestured for Amani. "I have had enough. Send me back to the city."

Gwandoya departed through the portal, leaving Maram alone with Amani. She sagged against the djinn. "Each time I see him, I dislike him more, and I hated the man on sight. When will he give up?"

Amani shook his head. "He is crazy in ways that few men are. He is not the sort to give up easily, or at all. The question you should be asking is: what will that madman do when he finally loses patience with you? I have no desire to harm you, but I am the slave of the lamp. Should he order me to kill you, I'm not sure I could disobey him. And your mother's shade would never forgive me."

"My mother is not dead."

Amani's mouth dropped open. "Briska

lives?"

Maram had never seen a man look as hungry as Amani did now. "She does. All my life, I was told that she'd been executed, as had you, but it turns out my father couldn't bring himself to kill her. He loved her too, you know. She is enslaved to something, just as you are, though I know not what or where. Only that she lives."

"One day, I wish to be free to find her."

Tears filled her eyes. "I hope one day you find her, too. You deserve to be happy."

"Your father would not think so."

"He will when I tell him how you have protected me here. If it weren't for you, I should have gone mad on that first day, or been eaten by a lion. It is four weeks since I arrived here, and you have never allowed me to lose hope that one day I might go home." Maram stared at him fiercely. "When I see my father again, I will demand that he release you from slavery."

Amani's smile seemed pitying. "He cannot, Princess. It takes magic to break a magical binding."

She refused to be put off. "Then I will make him summon an enchanter powerful enough to break it for him. If I have to endure another day here alone – "

"But you are not alone, Princess. Not any more. Open the gates and see."

Maram followed Amani to the entrance hall, where he threw open the doors and pointed. "Look out over the grass," he said.

In the darkness, she could see very little, but there did seem to be a faint glow, growing larger as she watched. Maram squinted. There appeared to be two figures, each carrying a torch. "Who are they?"

Amani's enigmatic smile told her nothing. "Wait and see."

It took an eternity for the two men to cross the flat plain to the gates. Maram didn't dare go out to meet them – in the weeks she'd been here, wild animals had picked Hasan's bones clean, and the bleached bones outside the gate were a warning of what the lions would do to her if she tried to leave.

The night breeze plucked at her veil, chilling Maram, but she simply folded her arms across her breasts and hugged what warmth she had left. If she went back into the palace for a shawl, the visitors might disappear, never to be seen again.

Finally, the figure came close enough for Maram to discern details. One man, not two, and he was cloaked against the cold, carrying a torch to light his way.

"What's that?" a familiar voice asked, lifting his torch to illuminate what remained of Hasan.

Maram's heart leaped for joy. "It was Hasan," she said, stepping forward out of the shadows. "They killed him and gave his body to the lions." She could feel tears threatening to fall. "I closed the doors, but I could still hear the bones cracking while they ate him. I have never been so alone as I am here. Then he comes at night and tries to seduce me – me! After I saw him kill Hasan!"

Aladdin set his torch in the bracket by the gate and ascended the steps. "You are safe now," he said, wrapping his arms around Maram. "I swear it."

Maram couldn't help it. Safe in his arms, she wept. For the senseless slaughter, the frustration of her own captivity, and most of all, for how much she'd missed this man.

"Everything will be all right. Tonight, we shall rest here, and on the morrow, I shall take you home," Aladdin soothed.

Amani cleared his throat. "You may go where you will, but the princess cannot leave."

A sob escaped from Maram, and the tears fell faster. "Please don't leave me, Aladdin. I cannot bear to be alone here again."

"I won't leave without you."

Never had the sensation of someone stroking her hair felt so exquisite.

"My master will return tomorrow night, and if he finds you, he will command me to kill you like Hasan, there," Amani said.

"But I am the master of the lamp," Aladdin said.

"Not any more," Amani said. "Gwandoya is my master now. And unlike you, he keeps the lamp safe on his person at all times, not in some alcove where anyone could see and steal it."

"But who would steal an old lamp?"

Amani sounded disapproving. "Anyone who knows its true worth. To have a powerful sorcerer like me at their command is something many would kill for."

"Gwandoya has already killed many men to get his hands on that lamp, and I was nearly one of them. There is no telling what he will do with such power." Aladdin sounded determined. "We must get it back."

"Nothing will make him surrender something so precious while he lives."

Maram raised her head and wiped her eyes. "Then Gwandoya must die. I won't let him kill Aladdin."

"Princess…" both men began.

She held up a hand to silence them. "I know I am not a fighter. I am a diplomat. But I have other weapons, and I'll be damned if I let him win. Tomorrow Gwandoya will die, and then I will get to go home. Are you with me?"

It took several hours and all Maram's powers of persuasion to get Aladdin and Amani to agree to her plan, but they did. The moon had reached its zenith, turning the jewelled garden into a sparkly paradise, as Amani took the hint and left her alone with Aladdin.

There were no tears when they came together this time, only kisses and increasingly urgent caresses. "Make love to me," Maram begged. She, who had never begged a man for anything in her life.

"When we are safely home and wed," Aladdin promised, stealing her breath with another kiss.

"Now!" she insisted. "Tomorrow anything could happen. Either of us could die, or he might escape with the lamp and leave us here, stranded. Tomorrow is uncertain, but I need to spend tonight in your arms."

She expected him to argue more, but all he said was, "As you wish, Princess."

Hardly daring to believe her luck, Maram led him to her bedchamber, where she eagerly peeled off her clothes. She turned, wanting to feast her eyes on Aladdin's body before she touched him. She had waited a long time for this.

"Why aren't you undressed?" she asked. Stepping forward, she seized the hem of his tunic. "Here, let me help you."

Gently, he pried her hands off his clothes. "No, Princess. I made you a promise and I intend to keep it. I swore I would set you free from your slavery, and I will. Your body is not a plaything for men to use for their own pleasure. You are the most beautiful woman I have ever seen and you deserve more, far more, than I can ever give. I love you, and I will take whatever pleasure you are willing to give me when you are free. Which you will never be, until we are wed."

"But you said…"

He gathered her up in his arms and carried her to the bed. Then he lay beside her, pulling her body against his, wrapping one arm around her breasts while his other hand rested on her belly. "I will hold you in my arms, like I said, and for now, I will be content."

She squirmed. "And if I am not? What about what I want?" She seized his hand from her belly and guided it between her thighs. "I want you, Aladdin. I am wet with anticipation, wanting the pleasure I will only feel when you are inside me."

His free arm tightened around her breasts. "Are you sure?" His voice was hoarse in her ear.

"Of course."

The words had barely left her lips before his fingers speared deep inside her, stroking all the right spots to make her gasp.

"More?"

"Oh yes!"

He hooked his leg around hers, anchoring her more firmly to his body as his fingers worked what could only be described as magic. One perfectly-placed circle of his thumb tipped her over the edge, sobbing his name.

He kissed the back of her neck. "Are you satisfied now, Princess?"

"Never!" she declared, then squeaked as his

fingers moved within her once more, stroking passion-inflamed flesh to another irresistible climax. She bucked, but he held her firmly in his arms, intent on her pleasure, even as he ignored his own growing arousal digging into her back. "You want me. I can feel it."

He laughed softly. "I don't just want you. I love you, and I desire you so much it hurts. But the only pleasure I will take in your bed tonight is yours." Again, his fingers stroked her, finding her most intimate places and making them sing.

Until…until…

"Aladdin, oh, how I love you!" she screamed.

Thirty-Two

"Something has changed. You are not as dejected as you were yesterday," Gwandoya greeted Maram, eyeing her with suspicion.

No woman could be dejected after a night experiencing the magic Aladdin could work with his fingers. The thought of what he might do with the rest of his body and hers was more than a little distracting. Not to mention frustrating, for he refused to give her more yet. That's why she'd spent the day leafing through the scrolls and books among her mother's things, looking for more information on djinn enslavement. After all, her mother had been a witch, too, with powers as limited as Maram's own.

"I miss having a man in my bed," she said honestly. "I have decided it is time to look to the future, and what you can give me. I have no maidservants here, and I have not had a new gown in weeks!"

Gwandoya's eyebrows rose, but as she spoke more fervently about maids and gowns, the suspicion in his expression slipped away. The man almost smiled.

He clapped his hands. "This calls for a betrothal feast. Bring us plenty of food and wine, for we will need it while we discuss our wedding."

Amani bowed and disappeared. Off to get what Gwandoya had asked for, no doubt. And what she had asked for, too.

Maram braced herself for what would be the biggest negotiation of her life, as she and Gwandoya argued the terms of a marriage she had no intention of entering into. Servants and jewels, palaces and gowns – for Gwandoya boasted that Amani could build her a palace anywhere she wanted, made of anything she pleased.

In the middle of Maram's lengthy deliberation of whether to have a stone castle far in the north, surrounded by blackberry hedges, or a palace like this one overlooking the sea, Amani brought a jug of wine.

"The finest vintage from the Sultan's own vineyards, which have lain in his cellar for more than a century," Amani announced, pouring cups for them both.

Maram's eyes lit up. "Ooh, is this the wine I told you about?"

Amani bowed. "Yes, Princess, it is."

She sipped, and scrunched up her face. The opium tasted as bitter as she had expected. "It does have a bite to it. Keeping it in a cellar for a century must do that, I suppose. But there is no better wine to toast our union with." She lifted her cup. "To our health and happiness, my lord."

Gwandoya preened, probably at the

unearned title. He lifted his own cup. "To our health and happiness indeed." He drained his cup, then smacked his lips appreciatively. "Tis strong stuff. Too strong for a woman, especially one who is about to become my obedient wife and bear my sons." He snatched up her cup and drained that, too, before commanding Amani to pour more for himself alone. "We shall start tonight."

Maram stared at him in shock. His calculating eyes regarded her over the rim of his cup as he gulped more wine, daring her to object. Obedience had been one of the things she'd traded for…something. If it meant he drank more of the drugged wine, then she would not argue. "Yes, my lord," she said, ducking her head in fake submission.

An idea struck her. "I have the perfect idea for my wedding gown. I would like seven layers of silk…" She described in excruciating detail one of the gowns she'd seen on the Queen of Beacon Isle, changing her mind about the colour only to return to the original shade as she saw Gwandoya's eyelids drooping.

Sleep, you mad bastard, she thought, pasting a smile on her face as she began a long debate about the merits of the exquisitely detailed painted shoes in Kasmirus compared to the silk slippers found in the bazaars closer to home.

"A good embroiderer can do just an intricate design with thread as a painter can with pigment, but there are few painters in Kasmirus who are talented enough any more. The royal family has a pair of christening shoes that have been in their family for generations, the most beautiful pair I have ever seen…"

Gwandoya's head flopped forward into a bowl of the bugs he liked so much.

"My lord?" she enquired. "Gwandoya?" She called his name several times, before gesturing for Amani to check him. She had no intention of touching him.

Amani eased Gwandoya's face out of the bowl and laid him on the floor. "He sleeps, but he still draws breath," Amani reported.

May heaven forgive her, but she had not been able to bring herself to kill the man, even with poison. Maram breathed out a sigh of relief. "Bring me the lamp."

Amani folded his arms across his chest and shook his head. "I cannot." His tone softened. "A new master of the lamp must take it from the old. I cannot choose who I serve."

"Fine." She rose and leaned over Gwandoya's sleeping form. The detestable man let out a loud snore. She reached into his tunic and pulled it from the grimy pocket where he kept it. Maram cradled the lamp in her clean hand while wiping the tainted one down the side of his tunic. Time to see if the old books were right.

A cloud of smoke surrounded Amani as he swelled to his full height, the impressive bulk of a djinn greeting his new master for the first time. "What is your wish, mistress?" he boomed.

"Take me, and everyone and everything inside this palace, back home where we belong." Remembering the first time, when she'd hit her head, she added, "As smoothly as possible, please, so that no one feels a thing."

"As you wish, mistress."

She felt the movement, little more than the sway of a ship at sea, before a slight bump told her they had arrived. A peep out the window revealed the shadow of buildings as someone carrying a torch ambled down the street. Maram was home.

"What else do you wish, mistress?"

"I wish to be free to marry the one I love, to be no man's slave any more."

Amani looked pained. "Princess, I cannot…"

Maram lifted her dagger from the table and sliced it across her hand. "I know. But I can. Blood of the betrayed that binds this djinn, my father's blood that runs in my veins, too, will set us both free." She seized the lamp in her bleeding hand, smearing the stuff over the blackened brass. "I am no man's mistress!"

Aladdin appeared. "Maram, no…"

She tossed the lamp at his feet. "Yes." She turned to Amani. "You are free. Find her, free her, and be happy."

Tears filled Amani's eyes, as, man-sized

once more, he bowed at Maram's feet. "As you command, Princess. When I find her, I will tell her that you have found happiness, too. If you ever have need of me, you have only to call, and I will be there to grant your wish." He touched her hand, and she felt the cut heal as though it had never been. Only then did Amani rise and incline his head to Aladdin. "Enjoy your palace. Consider it my wedding gift to the princess. But if you ever hurt her…know you will incur the enmity of the most powerful enchanter in the world. A man with no master. Not any more." He stuck a finger in his mouth, withdrew it, then traced a circle in the air. A portal opened, and he stepped through and was gone.

"Why did you do that? He was a traitor! The enslavement was his punishment for crimes even we do not know!" Aladdin's wild eyes reminded Maram of Gwandoya.

"I know. His only crime was to love my mother, and win her love in return. Neither of us deserves to be a slave, serving a master who might use us for ill." She took his hand.

"Please understand."

Aladdin swallowed. "I admit I do not, but there is very little about you I do understand. You are a great mystery to me, Princess Maram, but one I intend to spend my whole life studying. As long as your father doesn't kill me first."

"Why would my father kill my husband to be?"

"He gave me a month to bring you and this palace back, or he would cut off my head. Tomorrow is the last day of my month."

Maram folded her arms. "Then we will see the Sultan now, and sort this out. Next week is our wedding, and I want you alive."

Aladdin laughed. "I want you every bit as much as you want me, Princess. As you wish it, so must it be. To the Sultan's palace we go."

Thirty-Three

Sleepy servants showed Aladdin and Maram to an audience chamber, promising to tell the Sultan of their arrival. Time ticked by with no sign of the Sultan, as Maram dozed in Aladdin's arms and he found he didn't mind being kept waiting. No matter how many times Aladdin told himself he wasn't worthy of any princess, let alone Maram, the rightness of her body against his was undeniable. And the way her body had responded to him last night…she genuinely wanted him. Him,

Aladdin the humble spinner's son, briefly the master of a lamp and its djinn, but now…now he was just a man in love, waiting to beg the Sultan to spare his life so that he might marry the man's favourite daughter.

The first rays of sunlight entered the audience chamber before the Sultan marched in, his brow furrowed with annoyance. "What kind of man wants to be beheaded before I break my fast? If you weren't going to be executed today anyway, I would think up a suitable punishment for waking your Sultan too early."

Aladdin's first instinct was to prostrate himself at the Sultan's feet, but that would mean waking Maram, so he did not move. Instead, he said softly, "I know of no man who wishes to lose his head before you break your fast, Your Majesty. But I did not dare sleep until I had reported to you, as I promised." He stroked Maram's hair. "The princess made no such promise, though, so perhaps we should let her rest."

The Sultan's eyes widened. "You brought

her back? Is she hurt?"

"Not that I can tell, but she was kidnapped by a madman and held captive for weeks. There is no telling what he did to her."

"Where is the madman now?" the Sultan demanded.

"In the dining hall of my palace, unconscious. Your Majesty is welcome to him," Aladdin said.

The Sultan ordered two guards to bring Gwandoya back, then sat across from Aladdin and stared at him for a moment before he said, "For saving her, I would offer you her hand in marriage, if I had not already promised it to you."

Much though Aladdin would have liked to be the hero, he knew he didn't deserve the title. "She saved herself. She drugged her kidnapper's wine. The only reason she didn't do it earlier was because she did not think she could escape until I arrived. Your daughter is an amazing woman, and while I have no idea how I have managed to win her affection, I know I am the luckiest man alive."

"Indeed you are. She is everything a man could wish for, but will never attain." The Sultan sighed. "Just like her mother."

Aladdin longed to ask for the Sultan to say more, but as the silence stretched between them, he could not bring himself to do so.

"Your Majesty, the man you wanted."

The guards unceremoniously dumped Gwandoya on the floor.

"Wake him," the Sultan commanded grimly.

The guards tried shaking him, slapping him, then throwing a bucket of water over the man, but still Gwandoya did not wake. Then one of the guards bent over him and pressed a hand to Gwandoya's chest, over his heart. After a moment, the guard shook his head.

"He's gone, Your Majesty."

"What do you mean?" the Sultan asked.

"He's dead."

Maram stirred. "Serves him right for stealing my wine." She eyed Gwandoya's corpse. "Far too easy a death for the man who kidnapped me and killed Hasan. Throw his body into the gutter, to be devoured by stray dogs. It is no better than he deserves."

The Sultan sagged in relief at the sound of her voice. "Whatever you wish, Maram. We will postpone this wedding until you are well, and you shall have your apartments here so that my guards can keep you from further harm."

"No." Maram struggled to sit up, then aimed a glare at her father. "I will live in the palace my husband gave me, with him, and I will marry him on the morrow. Anyone who seeks to steal Aladdin from me again will suffer a worse fate than him." She pointed at Gwandoya.

The Sultan looked taken aback. Then, slowly, he said, "Whatever you wish."

Thirty-Four

Maram had attended many feasts in her life, but she never wanted one to finish as much as her wedding feast. Courtiers gushing over her dress, fawning over Aladdin, or exclaiming over delicacies they had never tasted before barely registered in her thoughts, for all that occupied her mind was the man beside her.

Finally, the Sultan commanded the guests to form a triumphal arch for the departing couple, and she and Aladdin were allowed to leave. She ran beside him as though her feet had wings, through the arch and all the way home. Guards stood at the gates now, a gift from her father, but she had eyes for only one man. A man whose hand she held tight in her own as she led him to the best bedchamber, a room she had not entered until now.

An enormous bed occupied most of it, piled with enough pillows and coverlets to sleep a small harem, for it was a bed fit for a king. Fit for her pretend prince and her, certainly.

She paused only long enough to kiss Aladdin deeply before she started shedding her clothes, not stopping until the layers of silk and linen lay on the floor. She lifted her chin. "Now, you must make love to me," she said.

He laughed. "As my princess commands."

She shook her head. "I am not a princess any more. Not truly. I am your wife, and nothing more." She'd never felt so free.

Finally, he tugged his tunic over his head and left it with her clothes. "You are everything to me. A princess, a queen…a woman to worship. I would do anything for you, princess or no."

She smiled. "Then lie down."

Her eyes drank in every inch of his naked body as he stretched out on the bed, his head pillowed on his folded arms as he stared straight back at her. Her husband was no soft courtier, or over-muscled knight. No, he was lean and hard, with no extra flesh or muscle that a man did not need.

"I can't make love to you while I am here and you are over there," he said, beckoning. "Come here, my beautiful wife, so that I can show you just how much I love you."

She grinned and crawled across the bed, stalking like a lioness. "Two nights ago you had your turn. Now it is mine." With practised ease and considerable pleasure, she straddled him, guiding him inside her until he filled her completely. "Oh yes. This is what I've longed for. All those nights, I dreamed…"

"As did I." His hands curved around her hips, cupping her bottom, as he drove deeper inside her.

They moved together in perfect harmony, two parts of one glorious being, not stopping the first time she screamed his name, but when she felt her second climax building, he slowed.

"I cannot resist you any longer, Maram. I must...I must..." His words dissolved into a groan of pure pleasure as she clenched around him, catapulting her own body into another longed-for climax.

When she caught her breath, she finished for him: "We must do this every night we are together, for as long as we live."

Aladdin laughed, stroking his fingers across her breast. "You are stealing my wishes, just as you have stolen my heart."

She kissed him, long and hard. "Granting them, more like. With Amani gone, all you have is me."

The silver ring on his finger caught her nipple, sending a jolt through her. "You are all I ever need. I have nothing left to wish for."

She rose. "I wish for a bath. Will you join me in the bathhouse?"

"Only if you will grant a wish there that I have longed for since the day I met you."

Making love to Aladdin in the water. Maram

shivered in delicious anticipation. "Now who's stealing wishes?"

He lifted her in his arms and carried her to the bathhouse, and Maram sighed blissfully, knowing there was nowhere else she would rather be, and truly nothing else she could wish for.

About the Author

Demelza Carlton has always loved the ocean, but on her first snorkelling trip she found she was afraid of fish.

She has since swum with sea lions, sharks and sea cucumbers and stood on spray drenched cliffs over a seething sea as a seven-metre cyclonic swell surged in, shattering a shipwreck below.

Demelza now lives in Perth, Western Australia, the shark attack capital of the world.

The *Ocean's Gift* series was her first foray into fiction, followed by her suspense thriller *Nightmares* trilogy. She swears the *Mel Goes to Hell* series ambushed her on a crowded train and wouldn't leave her alone.

Want to know more? You can follow Demelza on Facebook, Twitter, YouTube or her website, Demelza Carlton's Place at:

www.demelzacarlton.com

Books by Demelza Carlton

Ocean's Gift series
Ocean's Gift (#1)
Ocean's Infiltrator (#2)
Ocean's Depths (#3)
Water and Fire

Turbulence and Triumph series
Ocean's Justice (#1)
Ocean's Trial (#2)
Ocean's Triumph (#3)
Ocean's Ride (#4)
Ocean's Cage (#5)
Ocean's Birth (#6)
How To Catch Crabs

Nightmares Trilogy
Nightmares of Caitlin Lockyer (#1)
Necessary Evil of Nathan Miller (#2)
Afterlife of Alana Miller (#3)

The Complex series
Halcyon
Fishtail

Mel Goes to Hell series

Welcome to Hell (#1)
See You in Hell (#2)
Mel Goes to Hell (#3)
To Hell and Back (#4)
The Holiday From Hell (#5)
All Hell Breaks Loose (#6)

Romance Island Resort series

Maid for the Rock Star (#1)
The Rock Star's Email Order Bride (#2)
The Rock Star's Virginity (#3)
The Rock Star and the Billionaire (#4)
The Rock Star Wants A Wife (#5)
The Rock Star's Wedding (#6)
Maid for the South Pole (#7)
Jailbird Bride (#8)

Romance a Medieval Fairytale series

Enchant: Beauty and the Beast Retold
Dance: Cinderella Retold
Fly: Goose Girl Retold
Revel: Twelve Dancing Princesses Retold
Silence: Little Mermaid Retold
Awaken: Sleeping Beauty Retold
Embellish: Brave Little Tailor Retold
Appease: Princess and the Pea Retold
Blow: Three Little Pigs Retold
Return: Hansel and Gretel Retold
Wish: Aladdin Retold